GHOST DOPE

TIERRE FORD

TIERRE FORD

ABOUT THE AUTHOR

At just 12 years old, I started selling drugs in the 6th grade—following the blueprint I saw in my own home. My father was both a dealer and a user, and by the 7th grade, I had bought my first car, was paying my mama rent, and buying my own school clothes.

That same year, the school system labeled me as "slow." They placed me in a remedial reading class—embarrassed me, honestly. I was ashamed. But I still kept my swag, my gold chains, my Starter jackets, and my game face. I was one of the most popular kids in school, but truth be told, I had stopped learning. I was only there to show off.

Then one day, my reading teacher—who I'll never forget—looked me in my eyes and said, "You don't belong in this class. You're smart. Don't let them label you." Her words stuck with me, even though my CRT test scores said otherwise.

At age 12 years old I became my neighborhood's youngest drug supplier. I started with 10 dollars, and I flipped that all the way to over $500,000. Me and my Dad link up dealing together supplying the market. I dropped out of high school in the 10th grade. I bought my mother a house with a pool in the backyard, purchased luxury cars, before I was locked up at 19.

At that point in my life, I had never read a full book. Not one. But my father always told me, **"The mind is the most powerful tool in the universe. Street sense and book sense together? That's unstoppable."**

So I gave books a chance.

It started with street fiction. Then history. Then business. Then biographies about powerful and wealthy people. I started seeing myself in those pages—not always in their polish, but in their ambition, their boldness. Then I read **Think and Grow Rich and As a Man Thinketh.** Those two books changed my entire mindset.

That's when I met my friend Cool Harris. I saw some of his writing on a notepad, and it rocked my world. I realized I had something to say, too. From that moment on, I picked up the pencil—and I've never looked back.

I earned my GED, took business and college courses, and started studying resilience. I discovered that, back in the day, Black people were once forbidden to read. There's even a saying: **"If you want to hide something from a Black person, put it in a book."** That became my fuel.

Now, I write both fiction and self-help books, covering everything from mindset and mental toughness to financial strategy and spiritual growth. I pour my soul into every page with one mission: to light a fire inside someone who's ready for change.

To everyone who's followed my journey—thank you. Let's set the world on fire with truth, with courage, with knowledge. Let's break every chain and every myth that says we don't read.

Peace—And Keep The Faith.

TIERRE FORD

PROLOGUE

The cell reeked of bleach, body funk, and the sour truth of bad decisions. Fluorescent lights flickered overhead, casting yellow halos on gray cinder block walls. Eight men, all shades of Black and brown, sat spread across the concrete bench that wrapped three sides of the holding cell like a trap with no hinges. No mattresses. No clocks. Just time—thick and heavy like southern heat.

An old head leaned back in the corner, ankles crossed, arms folded like a man who'd seen too much and felt too little. His name was **OG Lamont**, gray at the temples, eyes sunken but sharp, voice deep as the river, smooth as a jazz vinyl. He tapped a finger against the wall like a metronome, letting the silence simmer before he spoke.

"You know what Ghost Dope is, don't you?"

A young man named **Keem**, probably no older than twenty-one, looked up from the floor. Skinny. Face full of questions and scars. "Nah, I heard the name... but what does it mean for real?"

OG Lamont chuckled low, bitter. "Mean you sittin' right here, son. Mean you got indicted for bricks you never touched. Kilos that never existed. Just somebody word sayin' you moved weight... and that was enough."

"So they ain't gotta catch you with nothin'?"

Tone, dark-skinned and dread-headed, slid closer. He was built like a cornerback with eyes always scanning. "Wait. Wait. You sayin' no dope? Like... zero? How that stick?"

Lamont nodded slowly. "It sticks like a roach on flypaper, boy. Fed just needs one rat with a mouth full of memories and a grudge... and that's law. They call it 'ghost dope' 'cause it ain't never seized, never tested, never seen. It only *exists* when it's time to sentence you."

Keem looked sick. "That sounds like witchcraft."

"Worse," Lamont said. "It's the *system*."

The room went still. You could hear the buzz of the light, the distant echo of a slamming cell door down the hall. Then came the jingle of keys and the unmistakable click of authority.

The **metal door groaned open.**

Two **DEA agents** in pressed suits stepped inside. Clean-shaven. Badges dangling. One flipped a folder open, eyes scanning the group like a wolf among sheep.

"Derrick Morgan."

A man in the back stood up. Slim, caramel-toned, with fear tucked behind his poker face. He looked back once before stepping forward. They cuffed him lightly and led him out into the hallway.

INTERVIEW ROOM – 15 MINUTES LATER

The room was colder. Metal table. Two chairs. One camera in the corner blinking red.

Agent Ramirez sat across from Derrick, flanked by Agent Miles. No smiles. Just ink pens and pressure.

"We ain't here to waste your time, Mr. Morgan," Ramirez began. "We're here about *Jay*."

Derrick blinked. "Who?"

"Don't insult us," Miles cut in. "We know Jay was your connection. We know he ran dope through your block. We know you were gettin' it heavy."

Derrick exhaled slowly. "Man... Jay used to slide me five times a week."

"Five what?"

"Kilos," Derrick said quietly.

The agents sat up straighter. Ramirez scribbled something on the pad. "How long?"

Derrick looked down at his cuffed hands. "Fifteen months. Every Friday like clockwork."

Miles tapped his calculator. "That's... roughly *three hundred and twenty-five kilos.* Street value?"

"Damn near ten mil," Ramirez muttered.

They leaned in.

"You want time knocked off? Help us build the rest. What was Jay's full name? Who else was on the payroll? Give us routes, stash spots, anything."

Derrick stayed silent for a beat too long.

BACK IN THE HOLDING CELL – LATER THAT NIGHT

Derrick walked back in, face pale. The others stared. Nobody spoke.

He sat down hard, eyes red, as if the truth had bled out of him.

The door opened again.

A new man stepped in. Young. Nervous. Beige jumpsuit is too big for his frame. Paper in his hand. Eyes darting around the room like a corner boy on the run.

"What they get you for?" Lamont asked.

The young man looked like he'd swallowed a fist. "Ghost dope," he whispered.

"How much time?"

He swallowed again.

"160 months."

The room inhaled.

"Damn," Tone whispered. "That's thirteen years…"

Keem leaned forward. "What they say you did?"

"I only knew two people on the indictment. It had 22 names on it. They had no control buys. No wire taps. No money. No photos. Just word of mouth."

He dropped to the floor, knees buckling, back against the cold steel. His paper slipped from his fingers. The sentence circled in red ink: **Conspiracy to Distribute Controlled Substance – 21 U.S.C. § 846.**

The young man laid on the floor like hope had a body and it had just died inside him.

"I ain't even got caught with a bag," he said. "I just knew some names."

The cell went silent again.

No birds. No windows. Just men trapped in a slow bleed of justice.

Some are waiting for trial. Some are hoping for a bond. Some weighing a plea.

But they all had one thing in common.

Ghost dope.

Dope that never existed—but stole their freedom just the same.

There are prisons filled with ghosts. Not of the dead, but of men condemned by memory, by words without proof, by laws without mercy. Ghost dope is the phantom that haunts the hood—and the system that makes it real.

In the end, it's not about guilt. It's about *cooperation*. And silence? Silence can cost you your life.

Welcome to *Ghost Dope*.

CHAPTER 1

Follow First Mind

The best thing you can do in this life… is **feel it first**.

Before the money. Before the pressure. Before people start clouding your judgment or numbers start lying to your heart.

They call it gut.

They call it instinct.

But really—it's your first mind. That quiet voice inside you saying: *this the move…* or *this ain't it.*

Most people ignore it.

Coach Jay didn't.

Coach Jay sat in his modest office, second-floor corner of the rec building, overlooking five baseball fields that glowed under late afternoon sun. His desk was cluttered with off-brand Gatorade bottles, rosters, scholarship pamphlets, and a half-eaten protein bar. A framed photo of last year's All-Star team leaned against a cracked plaque that read:

"It's Bigger Than Baseball."

He squinted down at a spreadsheet on his laptop when the door creaked open.

"Coach," said **Katey**, stepping in, a clipboard in one hand and a folder tucked under her arm. Blonde curls tied up in a bun, Target flats, clipboard queen of the booster moms.

Coach Jay looked up. "Talk to me, Katey."

She gave a sheepish smile. "We need to go over numbers. For the season."

Jay leaned back in his chair. "All ears."

She slid the folder on the desk. "Fundraising brought in just under $20,000. The goal was fifty. Still short thirty."

Jay nodded, not surprised. "I'll cover the rest."

Katey blinked. "Jay—are you sure? That's for all three teams. Travel, equipment, extra training... tutoring hours too."

Jay didn't flinch. "I said what I said. You can write the check."

She hesitated. "And the RV rental? Wasn't included."

Jay chuckled. "Probably just need one this year. For the East Coast trip."

Katey nodded, scribbled something, and started toward the door—then paused with a smirk. "How was the boat party?"

Jay grinned. "We had a blast. Carlos turned fifty on a baseball field with champagne in hand and too much reggaeton."

Katey laughed and disappeared down the hallway.

Outside, Jay stood under the tin-roofed awning that overlooked the fields. Five teams were spread across diamonds—one doing hitting drills, another running fielding reps, the third jogging laps, sweat glistening on their foreheads like an early work ethic.

"Boom!"
A baseball cracked into the sky and cleared the left field fence.

"Another one!"

Coach **Love**—dark skin, long dreadlocks tied back, muscle-packed frame in a team hoodie—walked up from third base line, beaming like a proud uncle.

"Three of our boys hittin' it out the park today," he said, clapping Jay on the shoulder. "Got two strong lefty pitchers dialed in too. We got a **core**, bruh. I'm smellin' the World Series already."

Jay smiled. "Let's stay humble."

"I ain't humble when I see talent."

A voice chimed in from behind—smooth, flirty, unmistakable.

"Coach, just wanted to say thank you for buying all that equipment."

Jay turned. **Pebbles** stood there—caramel skin, tight black joggers, white tank top with rhinestone "#BaseballMom" across the chest. She was stunning, the kind that turned heads whether she tried to or not.

Jay gave a warm nod. "No problem. Your boy's been puttin' in that work."

Coach Love added, "Shaq hittin' bombs out there. Training y'all invested in definitely paying off."

Pebbles beamed. "Mmm-hmm. Shaq's been locked in. That hitting coach y'all brought in? Worth every penny."

Love winked. "Shaq in the MVP conversation this year. Real talk."

Pebbles waved goodbye with a soft sway in her hips.

Love watched her walk off and muttered, "Man… her fine ass."

Jay shook his head. "Don't go there."

"I'm just sayin' what you thinkin'."

"Focus, man."

Jay tapped his clipboard. "The battle cage is blocked out for us Wednesday. Five to eight. Make sure you get names of kids without a ride. The hitting trainer will be there again too."

Love nodded. "Bet. I'll handle that."

They both turned their attention back to the diamond.

One kid rounded third so fast he stumbled into the bag, scrambled up, and kept pushing while parents in the bleachers laughed and cheered.

"Let's go, Tay!"

"Atta boy!"

"Slide, baby, slide!"

Jay soaked in the energy. He lived for this. The smell of leather gloves. The ping of metal bats. Young boys become disciplined men in cleats and eye black. This was his mission.

His phone buzzed.

Princess – Incoming Call

He stepped to the side and answered.

"Hey, baby."

Her voice was smooth, firm. "You still thinkin' about buyin' them two deluxe lots?"

"I'm with it. Do your magic, Boss Lady."

"Already done. I'll send the wire from the company account."

Jay chuckled. "You stay movin' like a CEO."

"That's 'cause I am. And don't forget—we got reservations tonight. Tom, Dick & Hank. Eight o'clock."

"I'll be ready. Steak and hushpuppies callin' me already."

Princess hung up with a click.

Jay looked back at the field as the sun dipped lower. In the distance, kids kept hitting. Parents kept clapping. Coaches kept correcting. It looked like peace.

But peace was always temporary in places like this.

Especially when the shadows don't chase you.

They

You feel it first.

The shift in the air. The silence between laughs. The way a phone call hits different when it comes late.

Jay didn't know it yet—but something was brewing. Something that would turn uniforms into mugshots.

And names into numbers.

They called it **Ghost Dope**.

And it was already making plays behind the scenes.

CHAPTER 2

Same Page, Same Power

Family ain't just blood—it's alignment.

It's waking up with the same mission.

Dreaming in sync.

Building without arguing the blueprint every night.

The glue ain't money, rings, or even kids.

It's two people reading from the same page... even when the storm rolls in.

Tom, Dick & Hank was dimly lit, soulful, and humming with laughter. Thick wood tables, warm jazz spilling out the speakers, smoke-kissed walls, and the scent of lemon pepper and bourbon glazed ribs floating like temptation in the air.

Princess sat across from Jay at a corner booth tucked under a mural of Black Atlanta legends. Her black satin blouse hugged her curves just right, her locks pinned up high, soft gold hoops gleaming against her cheekbones. She held up a glass of water, chilled and garnished with lemon.

Jay smirked and raised his tequila shot, rim salted and untouched until now.

"To life," she said, tapping his glass. "To health. Wealth. And this beautiful tiny creature in me."

Jay's eyes softened as he leaned back, hand drifting to her stomach. "You sure you are not just full from them hushpuppies?"

Princess smirked. "Don't play. You know what it is."

Jay downed the shot. "Ain't nothin' like peace of mind. Over eighteen months out of the game, not lookin' over my back? This right here? Just the beginning."

She sipped slowly. "You earned it. We earned it."

Their food arrived—his smoked salmon and garlic mash, her jerk chicken with pineapple slaw. The plates were hot and generous. A candle flickered between them like a promise.

"So tell me," she said, sliding a piece of plantain off her fork. "What's the next play? I know you are always cooking."

Jay nodded. "Property, no question. I want them two deluxe lots we talked about. One for long-term hold, the others we flip before summer ends."

"Mm-hmm. Already started the paperwork. They are building a new charter school by that intersection too. That's gonna spike the value."

Jay leaned in. "And the ball teams—Shaq hittin' over the fence now. Got two lefties throwin' smoke. Might hit the World Series this year."

Princess smiled. "You really saved them, boys, Jay. Like... gave 'em a shot at somethin' better. You should see how their moms talk about you at the salon."

"I ain't lookin' for praise. Just tryna reroute a few GPSs, that's all."

They both laughed, then she turned serious.

"You see what's goin' on though, right? They buildin' another prison, Jay. That means something. Meanwhile, the only damn park in that zip code just got shut down."

Jay sighed. "Yup. They goin' off their third-grade test scores again. Labelin' 'em before they even know what they are good at."

Princess shook her head. "Ain't no mystery. It's a damn business model."

Right then, **Hank**, the restaurant's owner—a burly man in a linen shirt and suspenders—walked over with a wide grin.

"Look who I see makin' power moves," he said, dapping Jay and giving Princess a gentle side hug. "Y'all glowing tonight."

Jay laughed. "Tryna stay out the way and stack somethin', that's all."

Hank pulled up a chair. "That's what I like to hear. You know we just broke ground on that football training facility down off Metropolitan?"

Jay nodded. "Heard about it. Falcons gonna be pullin' talent straight from high school now, huh?"

"Exactly. Whole pipeline strategy. This city is evolving fast. BeltLine expanding. Developers scoopin' everything east of the zoo. If y'all got your eyes on property—don't blink."

Princess looked over her glass. "That's what we just talkin' about."

Jay added, "Tryna secure before they start naming the blocks after coffee shops."

Hank slapped the table. "Man, say that again! I grew up on Harper Street. Now they callin' it *'Harper Village Commons'*—and rent is triple what it was five years ago."

They all shook their heads.

Jay leaned back. "That's why we plantin' flags now. Own somethin'. Build somethin'. Even if it's just a baseball field and a duplex."

Hank nodded and stood. "Keep doin' what y'all doin'. You makin' it harder for them to erase us."

As he walked away, Princess reached for Jay's hand.

"This baby… our next property… the team... I just want to stay in this space. No noise. No drama. Just growth."

Jay squeezed her hand. "That's the goal. But peace always comes with a price."

Princess gave a half-smile. "So long as we don't pay in regret, I'm good."

Jay looked past her toward the street outside, where a siren wailed in the distance. He didn't flinch. But he felt it.

That old feeling. Like something in the air just changed.

Being on the same page doesn't mean the story won't twist.

It just means, when it does—you ain't alone.

But sometimes peace ain't the beginning of freedom.

Sometimes, it's just the quiet before a name gets whispered in the wrong ear…and Ghost Dope rises from the shadows.

CHAPTER 3

Plots in Motion

They've already built the case.

Before the knock. Before the wire. Before you ever got that feeling in your gut.

Plots were made against you while you were sleepin'.

A case has been built without your fingerprints—just whispers, lies, and rehearsed testimonies.

You walkin' around clueless…

while behind closed doors, they write your future in **indictment ink**.

Back in the county holding cell, **OG Lamont** sat on the steel bench with his back against the cold wall, watching the new generation of faces walk in like lambs to a silent slaughter.

He cleared his throat. "Let me tell y'all how they *really* do it. The feds don't need no video. No phone taps. Hell, they barely need a crime. They just need a *story.*"

Keem, **Tone**, and the others leaned in.

"It starts with the grand jury. That's their favorite weapon. You don't get no lawyer in there. Ain't no cross-examinin'. Ain't even got to tell you they're using your name."

Tone asked, "So they just put anybody up there to talk?"

♻ 15 MONTHS EARLIER – FEDERAL COURTHOUSE, NORTHERN DISTRICT OF GEORGIA

The courtroom was sealed. Private session. Grand jury hearing in progress.

A **balding white man** in a dusty mechanic's shirt took the stand—nameplate read: **James "Jimmy" White**, 47, truck driver out of Birmingham, Alabama.

U.S. Assistant District Attorney **Howard Creighton**, a wiry man with slicked-back hair and wire-rim glasses, stepped up.

CREIGHTON: "State your name for the record."

JIMMY: "James White. But folks call me Jimmy."

CREIGHTON: "Occupation?"

JIMMY: "I haul freight. Drive rigs. Been doin' it since I was twenty-two."

CREIGHTON: "Mr. White, you're testifying today under a limited immunity agreement. Do you understand?"

JIMMY: "Yeah, I do."

CREIGHTON: "Tell this grand jury what you've been transporting, and for whom."

Jimmy glanced at the jury—nine white, three Black, one Hispanic. A school librarian, a retired Air Force tech, a mid-level Home Depot manager.

JIMMY: "Started off small. Back in 2008. Pickin' up packages in Houston. From a man named **Carlos Alvarez**. He said they were goin' to Atlanta."

CREIGHTON: "How much were you paid?"

JIMMY: " at first twenty thousand later Hundred thousand flat. Per week."

CREIGHTON: "And what exactly were you hauling?"

JIMMY: "Cocaine. Packed in truck beds. Usually 250 up to 500 kilos per trip. Half went to Atlanta. The other half went to Florida—Tampa, to a dude, folks called him *Slim*."

Creighton lifted two photographs—one of a warehouse on the west side of Atlanta, and one of a custom-painted semi-truck.

CREIGHTON: "This warehouse. Who did you deliver to there?"

JIMMY: "A tall brother named **Carl**. He ran logistics for a dude named Jay. Real low key."

CREIGHTON: "Have you ever met this 'Jay'?"

JIMMY: "Nah. Just heard his name. Folks respected it. Feared it, too."

⚖ FEDERAL COURT – TWO WITNESSES ALREADY INCARCERATED

A guard escorted Damon **"Dice" Richards**, 38, doing a 7-year stretch in South Carolina.

Creighton stood again. "Tell us how you know **Jay Collins**."

DICE: "Met him through a mutual back in 2012. Name was **Quincy Bell**. Jay moved carefully. But he had weight. Real weight."

CREIGHTON: "How long were you purchasing narcotics from him?"

DICE: "Over a year. Ten kilos every two weeks. Cash."

CREIGHTON: "Did you ever witness others doing business with him?"

DICE: "Only heard talk. Word moved fast."

Next up, **Leonard "Len" Carmichael**, 41, orange jumpsuit from another federal yard. He walked slower, voice steadier.

CREIGHTON: "Mr. Carmichael, same question. How did you meet Jay Collins?"

LEN: "At a strip club in Atlanta. Blue Flame. Back in 2011. We both were in the VIP throwing money. It was our birthday. We started talkin' numbers and weight."

CREIGHTON: "You bought narcotics from him?"

LEN: "Two years straight. As long as you paid, he came through."

⚖️ DEA + DA STRATEGY SESSION – BACK ROOM

DEA Special Agent Marcus Evers paced the hallway with DA **Creighton** and Judge **Myra Langford**, a sharp-eyed Black woman in her late fifties with no time for fluff.

EVERS: "We got testimony. Regular pattern. Multiple witnesses. Same names. Same drop points."

JUDGE LANGFORD: "But you still got no wires. No phone intercepts. No physical surveillance of Jay himself?"

CREIGHTON: "He's a ghost. No photos. No fingerprints. No money trails."

LANGFORD: "Then I'm not signing off on your warrant. You want a wire? Bring me hard connects. Not recycled convicts and truckers with a story."

Creighton frowned. "The system lets them move like this. He's cleaner than most lawyers."

Langford tapped her gavel softly. "You've got enough to build heat. But not enough to light the fire. *Not yet.*"

🎞️ JURY REACTIONS

Mrs. **Eleanor Pruitt**, 66, retired teacher, clutched her notepad while shaking hands. "They said they never *saw* the man…"

DeShawn Banks, 28, barista from East Point, leaned to the juror beside him. "I need more than stories, bruh. I ain't convictin' on hood legends."

But the seed was planted.
A name repeated.
A reputation laid bare.
They were drawing **shadows into people**...
And calling them facts.

⬦ BEHIND THE SCENES – DEA FILE ROOM

Inside a sealed envelope labeled: **"PROFFER: "Teddy Love"**, a full written statement sat untouched in a locked cabinet.

Filed by Agent **Marcus Evers**.

Dated **July 2013**.

It wouldn't be used until years later.
But it was there.
Waiting.

You think they build cases with facts.
But most of the time...
They build 'em with *faces*,
And they let the rest fill itself in.

Jay Collins' name had entered a courtroom he'd never seen.
And a conspiracy he'd never agreed to.

But once your name's on that paper...
Ghost Dope doesn't need a photo.
Just someone willing to swear they saw you near the fog.

CHAPTER 4

Whispers in the Fog

You ever feel like you are being watched... but don't see anybody?
 Like the shadows ain't movin', but your soul *knows* something out there?

Like your name bein' whispered just beneath the surface of silence... but you can't quite catch it?

That's the kind of fear that doesn't scream.

It sits quiet.

Heavy.
 Paranoia wearing church clothes.

You just prayin' by the grace of God your number ain't the one gettin' called next.

Sometimes the loudest place in the world... is your own mind.

The studio was live.

Not chaotic—**controlled chaos**. The kind that meant business was still booming. Smoke curled up toward the rafters from backwoods and papers, LED lights glowed purple across foam-padded walls, and a thick bassline rolled through the concrete floors like a heart that refused to slow down.

Inside **Level 3 Studios**, the vibe was electric.

Females twerked in crop tops and leggings, sipping Don Julio straight from red cups. A few white foam cups told you lean was in play. Somebody was rolling up again. Laughter. Sneaker squeaks. Auto-tune from the booth.

Then—

"Ay... Coach Jay just walked in."

The words floated out the booth through the engineer's mic. All heads turned. Eyes locked. Some were surprised. Others are respectful.

Jay nodded cool, like it was nothing.

He hadn't been there in weeks, but **his presence still carried weight**. Whether in the field or the streets, Jay Collins was someone people noticed when he walked in—even when he tried not to be.

Big Cheese—a husky dude in designer shades and a VLONE tee—made his way through the haze and gave Jay dap.

"Heard you were out the way. How was the trip?"

"Good," Jay replied. "But glad to be back. Atlanta got its own air."

Cheese chuckled. "Facts. Lemme catch you up."

They strolled past a group of producers locked into a beat pack on the screen.

"DG just locked in a feature with Bo Deal. Sold four beats to a crew outta Miami. And tonight—big one—he performing at the **Outkast DJ Showcase**. Whole room full of A&Rs, DJs, streaming execs. Big faces."

Jay nodded. "Say less. I'll be there. Gotta get out, shake some hands, rub some elbows."

Just then, a door creaked behind him.

D-Low slid in, wearing a scuffed leather jacket, eyes darting. Thinner than last time Jay saw him. Nervous energy in his step.

"Jay," he said, voice low. "Come here, man. Need to talk."

Jay followed him toward the back hallway near the sound vault, past crates of unboxed merch and unused mic stands.

"What's up?" Jay asked, already annoyed.

D-Low looked around before speaking. "I need you back in, man. It's ugly out here. People from outta towns are ready to pay whatever. Can't find any work. I'm sayin'—just point me to the plug if you ain't gon' touch it."

Jay squinted at him. "If you weren't my blood cousin, first—I'd think you were tryna set me up. Second—I'd toss your goofy ass outta here."

"C'mon, Jay—"

"Nah. I told you—I'm done. Finished. Stop comin' up here with that talk."

"I feel you. I do. But everybody ain't sittin' on a nest egg like you. Everybody ain't got real estate and streams of income and ball teams. Some of us are still stuck."

Jay stepped closer, eyes like daggers. "I told you. Stack and invest. You blew yours. Ballin', takin' trips, new cars, frontin' like you got it. Now you want me to pull you back in the fire I barely made it out of?"

"Cuz... at least point me in the right direction."

Jay shook his head. "You just don't get it."

He turned and walked off.

Back in the main studio, the debate was *heated.*

"Best rapper outta Atlanta right now?"

Hot Rod: "Easy. Future. Got classics. Got a vibe. Got hooks."

Bossman Drew: "Bruh, you stuck in 2015. Thugga runnin' this sh*t."

MO Hawk: "Ain't none of y'all mentionin' Jeezy? Disrespectful!"
DG (in the booth): "Ain't none of them touchin' 21 on this generation. Bars, beats, and branding."

A girl in biker shorts and a nose ring leaned in. "Y'all sleepin' on Lil Baby though. Boy got the flow, got the love, and the numbers."

Another one piped up from the couch, sipping out her cup. "I like Gunna. He talks rich but sounds sad. That balance is sexy."

Shawty Monee, petite with wild curls and black lipstick, smirked. "All of them are nice—but **y'all better remember what Outkast did** before you talk about who is the king of the A."

Jay chuckled from the corner, watching it all. This was culture. Chaos and rhythm. But beneath it all... a chill still crept up his spine.

He couldn't explain it.

Couldn't prove it.

But it felt like somebody was watching him from a corner that didn't exist.

You pray you are just paranoid.

But paranoia doesn't need evidence—it just needs a pattern.

A cousin shows up broke and desperate.

A room full of eyes goes quiet when you enter.

And suddenly... all the heat you walked away from?

Feels like it's walkin' back toward you.

Your name ain't been called yet.

But somebody out there already whisperin' it.

CHAPTER 5

Pressure Math

When more money goin' out than comin' in, your back stays pinned to the wall.

Every move gained weight.

Every breath feels taxed.

That's when the mindset starts to bend.

You still walkin', still smilin', still speakin' faith—but inside you just prayin' the math don't break you before the moment you break through.

And that's what it is:

Hope against Hustle.

One false step from either salvation or a cell.

The neon from **Outkast Studios** reflected off parked Benzes, black trucks with temporary tags, and low-riders freshly wrapped in chrome and candy paint. Inside, the air buzzed with Atlanta's finest—models, moguls, DJs, and dreamers. The walls dripped with gold records, graffiti tags, and red uplights that made every step feel like walking through flame.

Jay and **Bone** leaned against a hallway wall near the green room, drinks in hand, low conversation under loud trap beats.

Bone: "How was the party?"

Jay smirked. "Carlos put on a movie, no cap. Had body-painted females damn near naked, live crab boil in the courtyard, poker and blackjack tables inside. Hustlers flew in from LA, New Orleans, Detroit. Saw two cartel bosses just chillin'. Strip show in the back. Twenty-four-hour chef in the front."

Bone: "Damn. Sounds like a real Players Ball."

Jay laughed. "It was. But you know Carlos—he ain't throwin' that kinda party just for vibes. He tryna pull me back in."

Bone nodded, gaze heavy. "I won't lie to you, bruh. I've been *thinking* about it too. Right now, I got more money goin' out than comin' in. That math equals one thing."

Jay tilted his glass. "I feel that. I spent close to **a quarter million** on this music game. As of right now? Nowhere near makin' it back."

Bone nodded, silent for a moment. "Still... I'm holdin' on. Gotta believe all this sacrifice gon' pay off."

Jay looked out toward the stage area where lights were shifting. "You know what traps most of us in this game?"

"What?"

"We can't outlive our past. Bills chase us like a damn flu. No matter how many shots we take, we can't shake that fever."

"Real," Bone muttered. "How long has it been since them trucks got pulled?"

Jay looked him in the eye. "Over a year. Goin' on two."

"That was a bullet dodged."

Jay's jaw clenched. "Yeah... but you don't forget the sound of one flyin' past your ear."

Just then, the beat flipped in the main room. DJ called out—

"Y'all give it up for the one and only... **DG the Mannequin**!"

Lights hit the stage. The room surged. DG walked out in black leather pants, shirtless, chains dancing across his chest.

The beat dropped. A deep, trippy synth line.

♪♪ *"I paint pain like Picasso, heart cold as Roscoe's / Money come fast, still movin' like I'm hollow... / Devil on my shoulder but I moonwalk through potholes / Gotta keep a stick, never know who gon' plot though..."* ♪♪

Hook hit hard—

♪♪ *"Picasso with the pain brush / All I know is flame up / Mirror can't change us / Hustle 'til my name up..."* ♪♪

The crowd lost it.

Jay smiled—finally, a moment that *felt* like movement. Real traction. **Bad Smith**, DG's feature artist, came out for the hook, slick fade, voice melodic but gritty. They had a sound.

Big Cheese approached Jay mid-vibe, wearing a crispy Braves cap and diamonds that flashed under the stage lights.

"Jay, lemme introduce you to somebody."

He led him through the crowd to a tall man in an all-black fit, shades on indoors, rocking a high-top fade and polished presence.

"This right here is **Marcellus 'Cello' James**, PD at Vibe 97.3— number one station in the A."

Jay offered his hand. Cello gripped it firm.

Cello: "Heard your boy. DG got presence. I see it."

Jay: "Appreciate that. We just grindin'."

Cello: "We got a slot open next week. Prime time rotation. But ain't nothin' free. Clearance fee, first-run sponsorship. Fifteen."

Jay: "Fifteen thousand?"

Cello: "Correct. That's with intro spins, club drops, digital streams attached."

Jay hesitated. "Let's talk. Lunch. Tomorrow."

"You name the place," Cello said.

LATER THAT NIGHT – BACK AT THE STUDIO

Jay stood in the center of the booth with DG, Bad Smith, and two other artists. Pizza boxes scattered, ashtrays full, vibes mellow but focused.

"Ball in y'all court now," Jay said. "Don't get lazy."

DG looked up, eyes focused. "Coach, I'm locked. Keep me in the game. I'm runnin' all the way back."

Bad Smith: "This is the only time I feel alive."

Jay nodded. "Then remember this feeling. Remember your work ethic. Your mindset. That's what breaks ceilings. Not clout. Not drugs. Not luck. **Grind, discipline, and gas only.**"

They nodded, fire in their eyes.

LATE NIGHT – JAY'S HOME – BUCKHEAD

Princess sat at her desk, eyes locked on her MacBook, glasses on, hair tied up. She was editing a commercial reel for a real estate client, fingers flying.

Jay sat outside on the back deck under soft Edison bulbs, watching *Tubi* on a patio TV. Slippers on. Whiskey in hand.

Across the street, inside a parked sedan, **DEA Agent Marcus Evers** sat with a hot cup of coffee beside Agent **Joey Resnik**, the younger of the two, chewing sunflower seeds.

Evers: "He either got the best damn magic show goin'… or he really stopped hustlin'."

Resnik: "Could be. But you know the game. We can make a hundred mistakes. They only gotta make one."

Evers: "How much do you think he got in that house?"

Resnik: "If he's who they say he was? Nothin' less than a million."

Evers: "Patience, partner."

They both watched as Jay leaned back into his chair, eyes half-closed, unaware that every breath he took was being calculated.

Some battles don't come with alarms.

They build in silence, slow… like fog rising through cracks in your windows.

Jay didn't know tonight was being watched.

Didn't know men in suits were counting his future in digits and risk factors.

Didn't know patience could be weaponized.

But the house of hustle is always glass.

And the DEA?

They already got the rock.

CHAPTER 6

The System

The system wasn't built to be fair.

It was built to be efficient.

Built on bodies, bonded by lies, and balanced on paperwork.

They call it *justice*. But what it really is... is **a funnel**.

A slow-drip conveyor belt, greased with fear, bias, and bad deals.

You feed it one name, one accusation, one rumor turned statement...
and it spits out a *felon*, a *conviction*, and a *quota hit*.

Who benefits?

The ones writing the charges.

The ones funding the cages.

The ones building private prisons with taxpayer glue.

Who doesn't?

The ones born in zip codes already outlined in red ink.

The ones told they're guilty until they take a plea.

The ones who can't afford truth, because lies come cheaper.

And in this system?

Snitches don't just get stitches.

They get **rewards**.

Time cuts. Transfers. Immunity. Sometimes freedom.

Even when they lie...

Even when they never touched the man they named...

The government doesn't care.

As long as they get **who they want**.

🔎 UNITED STATES PENITENTIARY – SOUTH YARD

The air was thick with heat and murmurs.

Leonard "Len" Carmichael and **Kentucky Black** walked the track in slow, measured steps—jumpsuits halfway unzipped, shirts stained with sweat.

Kentucky Black: "So... you think you gon' get your time knocked down? Testifyin' on Jay?"

Len: "DEA told me once they bring him in, I'm straight. Said I'll be considered 'essential.'"

Kentucky nodded. "Man, I've been ear hustlin' too. I think I got me a story to tell. I know what kind of car he drivin'. I know where his momma stay. I know the whole nine."

Len (laughing): "Boy, they put you on that stand, jury gon' think you were his *best friend.*"

Kentucky smirked. "Exactly. I don't even need to know him—just need to sound like I do. Real ones too busy to defend their name, and that's where we slide in."

Len: "Now you gettin' the bigger picture. I never knew Jay either. But his boy? Big mouth. Told me everything. Strip clubs. Drop spots. Flossin' cash. All I needed."

Kentucky whistled low. "That strip club story? Genius. Can't prove or disprove it. Perfect grounds."

They passed a group of younger inmates doing dips on the pull-up bars. A group of females—CO trainees from the academy—stood beyond the wire fence watching, clipboards in hand.

Kentucky Black (grinning): "Soon as I knock off this 20-piece, I'm gettin' back out there. These women lookin' like a Friday night after payday."

Len: "Just play it right. Tell 'em what they wanna hear. Keep your eye on the prize."

They continued walking, same rhythm, same game.

One step closer to the reward the system promised—as long as someone else paid the price.

⊗ SOUTH ATLANTA – URBAN BATTER'S CAGE

The sound of baseballs cracking against aluminum bats echoed through the evening air. Jay stood just outside the fence, arms folded, watching the boys swing, hustle, run drills with bright eyes and raw talent.

Coach Love, sweatband on, clipboard in hand, strolled up beside him.

Coach Love: "You know what the best feelin' in the world is?"

Jay didn't answer, just looked his way.

"Wakin' up knowin' you here for your family. Ain't duckin' no knocks. Ain't worried about folks comin' to take you out of your life. Might not be rich, but we are free. And that means somethin'."

Jay nodded. "Ain't never felt this kinda peace. Stress used to ride my back like a second spine. Walkin' away from it? Best thing I ever did."

Love smiled. "Our reward comin', bro. Tenfold. I believe that. All the seeds we plantin'? They gon' bloom."

Jay's eyes drifted to the dugout where a boy caught a pop fly and threw it with clean precision.

"I just can't wait for Princess to drop my seed. That's all I've been thinkin' about lately."

Love: "You gon' be a great father. You already got the blueprint. Discipline. Presence. Purpose. You just gotta add love on top."

They bumped fists.

What they didn't see was the black Toyota Camry parked across the lot, tinted windows rolled down just enough for a lens to poke through.

Inside sat **DEA Agent Alicia Mendez**, early 40s, sharp-cheekboned, calm-eyed. Next to her, rookie agent **Travis Kent**, tapping a pen against his notepad.

Kent: "You believe he is clean?"

Mendez: "I don't know yet. He walks like a man who left it behind. But every hustler has a relapse point."

Kent: "don't matter at this point we have him by the balls we just hear see can he lead us to anybody else "

Mendez: "conspiracy and ghost dope some of the best laws some lawyers drawed up."

Kent: "Patience, huh?"

Mendez smirked. "Patience is a weapon. And we got time."

She raised the camera. Snapped three photos.

Jay.
The cage.

The scoreboard.

Evidence of a new life... or a disguise for the old one.

The system doesn't care if it's the truth or the tale.

The only thing that matters is if it leads to a cell.

You can be **coaching kids** or **walking the yard**—but as long as your name's in the air, your freedom ain't never guaranteed.

And for men like Jay Collins?
The trial has already started.

The jury just ain't in the courtroom yet.

CHAPTER 7

The Knock

When the door crashes in…everything you thought you knew buckles.

Not just the walls—but people.

The ones you trusted.

The ones who swore loyalty.

The ones you would've bet your name on.

Because the government doesn't need the truth.

All they need is the right picture—a convincing canvas made of lies, stitched together by "cooperating witnesses" and courtroom theater.

And time?

Time work two ways:

for you… or against you.

And sometimes the seconds that should've brought you peace…

 instead carry your name on the lips of the storm.

The night felt like something from a fairytale.

Jay and Princess had been in their own world—just the two of them.

The house glowed warm with low lights and soft music playing from the living room speaker. Etta James' *"Sunday Kind of Love"* hummed through the air, mixing with the aroma of smothered chicken, candied yams, and fresh cornbread that Princess had been plating on the counter.

Jay, barefoot and relaxed in gray sweatpants and a white tee, spun her gently in the middle of the kitchen.

Princess (laughing): "Boy, you got two left feet tonight."

Jay: "Two left feet that still pulled you though."

Princess: "Mm-hmm. You're right. I was just young and impressionable."

They danced through two full songs, playfully offbeat, her belly showing just enough to remind them both of the little heartbeat growing between them.

Later, seated on the couch with plates in hand, they tossed around baby names between bites.

Princess: "Okay. If it's a girl—Soleil. Like sunshine. French, elegant."

Jay: "And if it's a boy—what about Zaire? Strong. Royal."

Princess: "Zaire Collins... I like that. Got a ring to it."

They sipped sweet tea and leaned into each other, the kind of evening that felt untouched by the world outside.

Jay: "I been thinkin'... if this music thing finally hits, and DG album do numbers like we expect, we could invest in a creative arts center. Kids need that."

Princess: "You always got your mind on impact. That's what makes you dangerous in a good way."

Jay: "You know where I wanna be in five years?"

Princess: "Where?"

Jay: "Here. Still cookin' with you. Still dancin'. Watchin' Zaire or Soleil run through this living room while I complain about somebody spillin' juice on my rug."

They laughed.

Princess: "What color we painting the baby room?"

Jay: "Yellow. Unisex. Bright. Peaceful."

She kissed his cheek. "You gon' be an amazing father."

Then came the sound.

BOOM BOOM BOOM.

Three heavy fists to the door.

The plates rattled. Music still played, but only for a second longer.

"DEA! OPEN THE DOOR! FEDERAL WARRANT!"

Jay's heart slammed against his ribs. Princess froze mid-step, her fork slipping from her fingers and clanging against the plate.

"Jay…"

"Shhh—don't panic."

He darted toward the living room window, peeked through the curtain. Black SUVs. Flashlights. Vests.

"Oh my God…" Princess whispered, hand on her stomach. "Is this really—?"

"Get in the room. Now. Lock it. Don't open it unless I say so."

"Jay—what's happening? Why are they here?"

"I don't know. I swear I don't know."

CRACK!

The battering ram hit the front door. Once. Twice.

BOOM! The third time was the death blow.

The door flew open. Boots thundered inside. Voices screamed in stereo.

"DOWN! HANDS UP! DO IT NOW!"

Jay raised both hands, stepping away from the couch.

"I'm not resisting! My wife is pregnant! Chill out—"

"DOWN! FACE DOWN! MOVE AGAIN AND WE SHOOT!"

He dropped flat onto the hardwood floor, arms stretched wide. Princess screamed from the hallway. Two agents pushed past Jay and swept into the bedrooms.

"Sir, you are under federal investigation and detainment—do not resist!"

Cuffs hit his wrists with the kind of force that made him groan.

Princess emerged crying, her hands up. "Please! He didn't do anything! He's been clean! He's a coach! He's not—he's not who y'all think he is!"

They grabbed her gently but firmly, guiding her to a chair, checking her for weapons, ignoring her words.

Jay looked up at her from the floor, eyes wide, confused, breath shaking.

"Princess—I swear to God, I didn't do nothing. I don't know what this is…"

An agent leaned over him, reading off the warrant.

"Jason Collins, aka Coach Jay—you are named in a sealed federal indictment under conspiracy to distribute controlled substances, Title 21 USC 846."

Jay shook his head.

"This shit crazy. You got the wrong man."

The agent just tightened the cuffs.

"That's what they all say."

They don't knock when they come for you.

They crash.

They drag your life out by the throat and force it to kneel in front of a system that already wrote the ending.

You could be dancing one minute, naming your child the next— and still get painted into someone else's picture.

Because the truth doesn't matter when the frame is already built.

And at that moment...

Time didn't just turn against Jay.

It declared **war**.

CHAPTER 8

Past Due

Just when you been playin' it right—
Stackin' slow, lovin' hard, doin' the *right* things…
That's when the unexpected shows up like a ghost in daylight.

A knock.
A name.
A file with your face on it.

Because when the past don't stay buried—
it digs *you* up.
Turn your discipline into a headline.
And makes your *old life* your *worst enemy.*

Jay moved like a man underwater.
In a trance.
Breathin', but not feelin'.
Blinkin', but not seein'.

His wrists were still cuffed as they walked him down the hallway
of the **Federal Detention Center**, white walls and silence
stretching forever. Everything was slow—the buzz of the door,
the cold click of the gate, the way the floor beneath him didn't
feel like it existed.

But what haunted him wasn't the cuffs.
It was Princess's face.

Frozen.
Panicked.
Still wearing that soft yellow T-shirt she'd changed into after
dinner.
Mouth slightly open.
Eyes holding questions he couldn't answer.

They'd printed his hands. Taken his shoes. Stripped him down to numbers.

Now they brought him into a **small white room**—a single table, two chairs, and a camera light blinking in the corner.

Two agents entered.

Agent Marcus Evers sat first, leaning back with calm arrogance. **Agent Alicia Mendez** followed, cool and quiet, with a manila folder in her hand.

They slid a phone across the table.

Evers: "Pick it up."

Jay hesitated.

"We already recorded the call, Coach. Just do it."

He picked up the line.

A voice came through the other side—deep, firm, clearly prepped.

Voice: "Jason Collins, also known as Coach Jay. Let me confirm some facts. You run multiple youth baseball programs under the **Collins Elite Athletics Foundation**, correct?"

Jay swallowed. "Yes."

"You sponsor travel tournaments, provide tutoring programs, and own equity in **SouthEast Sound Studios**, correct?"

"Yeah."

"Your wife's name is **Princess Collins**, and you are expecting your first child. You reside at—"

Jay cut in. "Yeah. That's me. I'm not hiding who I am."

There was a pause.

"Do you know why you're here?"

Jay stared at the wall. "No."

Agent Mendez scribbled notes.

"What happened in April, Mr. Collins?"

Jay shook his head. "Nothing. April? That's... spring training. I was coaching."

Evers: "No. April 14th. Truck pulled over outside Augusta. Found 500 keys of coke."

Jay's face twitched.

"Do you know anything about that?"

Jay paused, forcing his voice flat. "No."

"You know a man named **Carlos Alvarez**?"

Jay blinked. "Can't say I do."

Mendez (leaning forward): "So you weren't at his party in January? You know... the one with the blackjack tables? The body paint? The chefs flew in from Mexico?"

The hit landed.

Like a gut punch.

Jay didn't flinch physically, but something inside him twisted hard.

He felt the memory rush in.
Carlos laughing.
Cameras flashing.
Bodypaint on brown skin and shrimp cocktail towers.
He remembered telling Bone, *"He's trying to pull me back in."*

It hit too hard to hide.

And in that daze—he said it without realizing:

"I want my lawyer present."

The room fell still.

Evers and Mendez looked at each other.
 Smiled.

CLICK.

The camera and audio recorder stopped.

📱 MEANWHILE – JAY & PRINCESS'S HOME

Princess paced the kitchen barefoot, heart racing, phone clutched to her ear. She was in a hoodie now, hair in a rushed bun, her plate from dinner still on the counter—untouched.

Princess: "They came in with full vests. Kicked the door. Said it was a federal warrant. Took him right in front of me."

On the other end, **Attorney Maxwell**, Jay's long-time lawyer and friend, sounded composed but concerned.

"Did they search the house?"

Princess: "No. Not really. Just checked him and went. Didn't flip anything."

Maxwell "Then this wasn't an active search. This is a pickup warrant—means a sealed indictment got unsealed. Something from the past. Something they *already built.*"

Princess sat down slowly. "Will he get a bond?"

"Could go either way. Depends on if they argue he's a flight risk. Give me a couple hours—I'll pull the case file, find out which judge, and call the AUSA handling it. Sit tight. You'll hear from me soon."

"Maxwell …"

"Yeah?"

"He didn't do anything. He's been clean."

"I believe you. That's why I'm on it now."

She hung up and stared at the front door—now dented and hanging slightly off its hinge.

The house was too quiet.
Too still.
And for the first time, she felt like the baby in her stomach could feel everything she was holding back.

The problem with the past is...don't ask permission before comin' back.
It doesn't knock.
It kicks in your door, smiles at your success, and throws handcuffs on your peace.

Jay didn't run.
He didn't hustle.
He didn't lie.

But in this system?
That doesn't always matter.

Because if they *want* you to be guilty—
They'll find someone willing to say you are.

CHAPTER 9

False Crowns

Stackin' up millions'll have you thinkin' you invincible.
Like you beat the game.
Like the law doesn't apply any more.
Like you found the cheat code and walked out the streets untouched.

But time...
Time is the best teacher of all things.
It doesn't yell.
Don't warn.
Just *keeps ticking*—
until one day you realize the clock had its own beat all along.

🔎 TAMPA, FLORIDA – 24 MONTHS EARLIER

The sun had just slipped behind the skyline, and the **Hard Rock Casino** parking lot buzzed with late-night energy. Neon reflected off chrome wheels. Reggaeton spilled from passing cars. But inside a blacked-out **Range Rover**, the tone was all business.

Carlos Alvarez, mid-40s, tailored black button-up, Cuban links, sat in the driver seat, flipping through a black duffel bag stuffed with bricks of rubber-banded cash.

Across from him sat **Drake "Slim" Wills**, Atlanta-born, Florida-based, lean frame, heavy watch, and sharp eyes. He looked like money. Talk like a legacy.

Slim passed Carlos the bag.

Slim: "That's the full load. No shorts."

Carlos zipped it up. "Appreciate you. But no more loads comin'. I'm out."

Slim raised an eyebrow. "Out out?"

Carlos nodded. "We had a good run. A few fumbles... nothin' we couldn't handle. But I'm done rollin' the dice. Especially after that crab table in Biloxi."

Slim chuckled. "Yeah, you got cleaned that night. Should've known not to bet against the old Black lady with the wig and lucky chips."

Carlos smirked, then leaned back.

Carlos: "I'm buyin' 25 acres just north of here. Buildin' my dream home. Gated. Got a stream runnin' through it. Other homes too— eight to ten units. Gonna name the whole subdivision after my wife. Street names? All my kids. Parents. Grandparents."

Slim looked out the window, nodded slowly.

Slim: "Damn. That sounds hard as hell. Lowkey genius. You're really on to somethin'."

Carlos grinned. "Puttin' up three millions of my own. Rest comin' through financing. It's a $ eight million dollar project."

Slim exhaled. "Man... I've been lookin' into real estate too. Flippin' some houses. Got my eye on two barbershops and a corner cafe."

Carlos pointed. "That's the key, bro. Money gotta grow. Not just spin."

Slim nodded. "True. But if all else fails..."

Carlos finished it: "We still got the streets."

They laughed. Dapped up hard. A brotherhood sealed in money, ambition, and shadows.

Across the lot, in a **gray sedan**, **DEA Agent Travis Kent** snapped a photo through a long-range lens.

Click.

Slim stepping out the truck.

Click.

Carlos is still inside.

Click.

The **license plate**. The **time**. The **duration** of conversation. The exact **distance between vehicles**.

In the passenger seat, **Agent Mendez** scribbled everything in a spiral notebook.

Mendez: "Ten minutes. Hand-off complete. That's the third time in two months."

Kent: "Slim. Carlos. And our mystery man… Jay Collins. We get all three, we rewrite the city's supply chain."

Mendez smirked. "We don't just want the money. We want the illusion. Crush their *happy drug-dealing world.*"

📍 SOUTH TAMPA – 8 MILES AWAY – SLIM'S HOME

Slim pulled into the driveway of a sleek three-bedroom home on a quiet cul-de-sac. Porch lights on. Palm trees lined the walk.

He stepped out with a **box of hot Krispy Kreme donuts**, still warm, and walked through the front door.

Sierra, his fiancée, sat on the floor with their two kids—one drawing with crayons, the other climbing her lap.

She looked up. "You made it back quick."

Slim kissed her forehead. "Yeah, I needed to."

He handed her the donuts, then dropped to his knees beside her. Looked her straight in the eye.

"I'm done."

She blinked. "Done?"

"Out. Fully. Me and Carlos shook hands tonight. No more loads. No more late calls. It's just us now. House. Business. Legacy."

Her eyes watered. "Are you serious?"

"Dead serious. We are building something real now. No more risk."

The kids climbed over them as they hugged—one big family huddle. Peace wrapped in sugar and second chances.

Outside, in another parked DEA car two houses down, Kent watched from behind dark glass.

Kent: "Look at that. Got his perfect little life. Donuts and lies."

Mendez leaned back. "They always think they're slick until we knock on the door."

"We have to connect Carlos Jay and Slim be a nice promotion for us ?"

The problem with stacking money in silence…if you forget who's listening.

You think you're clean, but the paper trail is still bleeding.

You think you made it out,

but your past doesn't need directions.

It already knows where you live.

And for Carlos, Slim, and Jay?

The clock had already started counting down.

CHAPTER 10

Wind and Roots

The wind blows…and the trees without strong roots?
They come down first.

They sway with temptation.
Bend toward easy money.
And when the pressure hits—they snap.

Because peace without purpose is a setup.
And when old hustlers try to wear new lives…even the breeze
feels like betrayal.

📍 TAMPA, FLORIDA – 6 MONTHS BEFORE JAY'S ARREST

Inside **Mendoza's Tuxedo & Tailor**, soft jazz played overhead
while three men stood on raised platforms, arms out, being
measured with the precision of a jeweler.

Slim stood in the middle—polished, clean-shaven, beaming.

To his left was **Rico**, his lifelong right hand, built like a linebacker
with a sharp fade and sharper smile. To his right, **Bud**, streetwise
and quiet, diamond stud in each ear, eyes always scanning.

Rico: "Man, I ain't gon' lie—the game been missin' us."

Bud: "Real talk. Streets are still void. Ain't nothin' but rerock
movin'. Boys waterin' down product and overchargiin'."

Slim smirked as the tailor adjusted his cuff length.

Slim: "That's what the streets do. It figures it out… eventually."

Rico: "Yeah, but right now? Man, we could slide in under the
radar and make a clean few million in six months."

Bud stepped off the platform, stretching.

"Legit money doesn't move like street money. That's the truth. These barbershops and vending machines ain't cuttin' it right now."

Slim: "Carlos just hit me too. Invited me to his 50th on the water. Yacht party, full layout."

Rico (smirking): "See, that's what I'm talkin' about. Big dog moves. But lowkey? We spendin' like we still touchin' that old weight. Ain't nothin' came back like it used to."

The three shared a look.

That unspoken moment where everyone was thinking the same thing... but waiting for someone else to say it out loud.

📍 UNMARKED SEDAN – PARKED DOWN THE STREET

Inside a **DEA stakeout vehicle,** two agents sat in silence—**Agent Travis Kent** sipping black coffee, **Agent Alicia Mendez** scrolling through surveillance logs.

Kent: "You believe it? They really might've gone cold turkey."

Mendez: "Slim ain't moved in months. Carlos livin' soft. Jay off the radar. It's like they flipped the script."

Kent: "So what's next?"

Mendez leaned her head back against the headrest.

"Next is patience. That's our favorite weapon, remember? They always circle back. Greed don't retire."

Kent smirked. "And the best part?"

"We don't have to catch 'em red-handed. We just gotta paint a picture that looks like they doin' what we say they doin'."

They both laughed quietly.

"Ghost Dope Conspiracy. Our best weapon Invited"

Kent nodded. "Truth doesn't matter when the whole canvas is dirty."

Through the windshield, they watched Slim and his crew exit the shop—sharp suits, big grins, clean cuts. Rico checked his watch, Bud stretched his arms, and Slim led the pack.

Slim (laughing): "So what we eatin'? I'm starved."

Bud: "mouth-watering now for Bern Steak house steaks thick as my arm."

Rico: "Let's ride. I'm feelin' like champagne."

As they pulled off in three separate blacked-out SUVs, the agents didn't follow.

They didn't have to.

They were already in position.

Already building their story.

Already counting days like poker chips.

They say if you leave the streets clean, you are safe.

But when the feds want you—

your past doesn't need to be present.

All it takes… is a whisper, a snapshot,

and a story told the right way.

Because in the world of **Ghost Dope**—you don't need evidence.

Just **expectation**.

And a little wind…to bring the whole house down.

CHAPTER 11

Closed Doors & Open Lies

Behind closed doors is where the truth dies slow.
 Not with bullets.
 But with *statements.*

The people you thought were solid?

They were never friends.

They were **fans of your downfall**—jealous enemies who clapped for you in public and pointed at you in private.

And the grand jury?

That's where the government lets lies grow roots.
No defense attorney.
No cross-exam.
No chance to correct what's said about you.

Just twelve strangers...
A prosecutor with a script...
And a witness with a motive.

U.S. DISTRICT COURT – NORTHERN DISTRICT OF FLORIDA

Two Years Earlier – Before the Case Was Public

Inside **Courtroom 4B**, the fluorescent lights hummed. No press. No open gallery. Just a dozen jurors—retirees, postal workers, a dental hygienist, a youth minister—spread out in worn chairs, legal pads in their laps.

Assistant U.S. Attorney Melissa Riggs, mid-40s, razor-sharp with an icy voice, stood at the podium. Her charcoal suit matched her tone.

"Next witness: Bobby Dale."

A door opened. **Bobby Dale**, 36, white male, buzzed head, tattoos on both arms, walked in cuffed. Prison-issued jumpsuit. Still had pride in his posture.

He raised his right hand. Swore in.

Riggs: "Mr. Dale, please state your full name for the record."
Bobby: "Robert Franklin Dale. Everyone calls me Bobby."
Riggs: "Mr. Dale, do you know a man by the name of *Drake Wills*, also known as *Slim*?"

Bobby: "Yeah. Been knowin' him for over five years."

Riggs: "Would you describe your relationship as social or criminal in nature?"

Bobby (shrugs): "Started socializing. Turned criminal."

Riggs: "Explain."

Bobby: "I started buyin' zips off him. Then weight. First a few ounces, then full bricks. Past couple years? I've been grabbin' five kilos a week."

Riggs (writing): "Every week?"

Bobby: "Every week. Rain or shine."

She paced slowly. Letting the gravity settle.

Riggs: "And this lasted how long?"

Bobby: "Little over two years. Up 'til I got jammed."

Riggs: "Did Mr. Wills ever instruct you on transport, payment, or security?"

Bobby: "He ain't talk much. But everything was organized. Clean. Cash drops. Same motel. Different cars."

Riggs: "Did you ever witness him conducting business with others?"

Bobby: "Not directly. But he'd leave me waitin' while he did runs."

Riggs nodded, satisfied.

"That's all for now."

She turned. "Next witness: **Kendra Mays**."

🔎 INSIDE COURTROOM – 5 MINUTES LATER

Kendra, mid-20s, light brown skin, long straight weave, wore a tight dress and platform heels even under subpoena. She swore in, flipped her hair once, then looked around at the jury with barely disguised nerves.

Riggs: "Please state your full name."

Kendra: "Kendra Renee Mays."

Riggs: "Occupation?"

Kendra: "Dancer. Was at Blue Flame in Atlanta. Then... Diamond Dolls in Tampa."

Riggs: "Do you know Drake Wills?"

Kendra (smiling): "Yeah. We messed around for a while."

Riggs: "What was the nature of your relationship?"

Kendra: "We kicked it. He'd come in, throw money. Took me out. Then I introduced him to my brother."

Riggs: "And what happened after that?"

Kendra: "They started dealin'. I ain't in it—I was just the link."

Riggs: "Do you know how much money exchanged hands?"

Kendra: "Not exactly. But one time I saw a bag—$320,000. Cash. I heard Slim say somethin' about buyin' weight."

Riggs: "How long did this business relationship go on?"

Kendra: "Close to two years. Before my brother got locked."

Riggs: "And in all that time, did Slim ever deny being in the game?"

Kendra: "Nah. He ain't never hide it."

Riggs: "Thank you, Ms. Mays."

Kendra stepped down, nerves melting into pride.

Outside, the grand jury sat motionless—but the dots were being connected.

📍 SLIM – MONTHS BEFORE JAY ARREST – GYM IN TAMPA

The gym echoed with squeaks and bouncing balls. Slim stood courtside, watching his son and other kids run drills. The coach barked out a play.

"Double screen! Swing the ball! Cut hard—finish at the rim!"

Slim clapped. Smiled. His son caught the pass and laid it in smoothly.

The phone buzzed.

Sierra: "Hey babe. Just left the venue. Cake tasting at 3. Don't forget."

Slim: "I won't. Gonna stop by mama's, then I'm all yours."

Sierra (laughing): "Don't come full from her sweet potato pie."

"No promises."

Another call.

Bud.

Slim: "Yo."

Bud: "All good. All the way good."

Slim: "Say less. Be by after I get done here."

🔎 OUTSIDE COURTHOUSE – DEA CONVERSATION

Inside the courthouse hallway, just outside the sealed grand jury chamber, **Agent Mendez** met with **Senior Case Agent Duval**— a white-haired Fed with a gravel voice and coffee breath.

Mendez: "We've got corroboration. Two witnesses. Timeline overlap. Confirmed funds. Language is consistent."

Duval: "Perfect. I'll get the judge to authorize the full nine— wires, cameras, banking surveillance. We're building the net now."

Another agent approached—Agent Cole.

Cole: "Just got confirmation—Carlos' financials came in. His shell company moved $3.4 million in twenty months."

Duval (grinning): "They're walking into this one. No fireworks. Just a slow, pretty noose."

Mendez: "Jay's still clean. That's the problem."

Duval: "That's the beauty. He *thinks* he's out. But if he so much as answers the wrong call, he's in."

Mendez exhaled. "We're about to make headlines with this."

Duval (smiling): "Let's give 'em a conspiracy so tight, they won't even have room to blink."

It's not what you *do* that gets you indicted.

It's what they say you did.

It's who they say you did it with.

And who's willing to nod on a stand to save themselves.

Because the **grand jury doesn't need your side of the story**.

It just needs a picture that *feels* true.

And the courtroom is a canvas...

where your enemies paint in the colors of your past—

with the feds holding the brush.

CHAPTER 12

Dry Wire, Loaded Dice

The streets will let you breathe long enough to make you think you're free.

But freedom ain't peace—it's patience.

And in the world of indictments and silence,

The absence of evidence doesn't mean you are off the hook.

It just means they waitin'...

for the perfect **mistake**.

📍 DEA FIELD OFFICE – ATLANTA DIVISION

Fluorescent lights buzzed overhead. The air smelled like coffee, toner, and low morale.

Senior Agent Marcus Evers paced across the open case board, arms crossed, jaw tight. Beside him, **Agent Alicia Mendez** flipped through transcripts stacked high with highlighted names and hearsay.

Evers: "Judge Langford just sent word. She won't sign off on *any more* wiretaps. Says we're chasin' shadows."

Agent Travis Kent, younger and more eager, leaned on the desk.

Kent: "We ain't had movement in sixteen months. Carlos is a ghost. Jay's silent. Slim's just—**floatin'**."

Mendez: "As of now, would this even hold up in court?"

Evers (shaking his head): "We got whispers. No bricks. No surveillance. No phones. Just... *stories*."

Kent: "What about the Augusta truck? 500 keys?"

Mendez: "Still no phone records linking Slim. The driver didn't have any phone records with them. No group pictures, no birthday parties. Hell no strip club outing together. Only one person can put all three in the room together "

A silence stretched. Heavy.

Evers: "Right now... it's *hearsay*. And hearsay doesn't close cases."

Kent sighed. "So what now? We pull 'em in?"

Mendez: "Not yet. We bring 'em in now, they 50/50 walk. The case needs something fresh, something just one dot that connects the rest of the story."

Evers looked out the window, city lights stretching forever.

Evers: "We lay low. Let one of 'em get sloppy. Let one *slip*. We got five years from the last drop to bring charges. The clock is still ticking."

Mendez nodded slowly. "And time is our friend."

🔎 TAMPA, FLORIDA – LUCKY 9 POOL HALL

Neon buzzed. Laughter spilled across the room. **Cigars. Whiskey. Hustlers. Loud bets.**

Slim, **Rico**, **Bud**, and a few others were circled around a corner table, each leaning in, watching two games run side by side.

Bud sipped from a glass and grinned.

Bud: "Bachelor party going be like somethin' outta Netflix, bruh making the history books."

Rico: "We talkin' jet skis? Islands? Or just a bunch of chicks we can't remember tomorrow?"

Slim (laughing): "All I'ma say is—it's gonna y'all make it big and right a player coming off the market. Just have it ready when I get back from Carlos' 50th Bday bash? "

They toasted. Glass clinks all around.

Torrey, thinner, with fading golds and tired eyes, leaned in.

"Man… been sixteen months without work. Pockets low. Hope y'all ain't talkin' just party. I'm thinkin' *business*."

Slim looked at him.

Slim: " Stop playing, if you think I'm 'bout to fumble for a quick flip—you better talk to yourself in the mirror first."

Bud nodded. "Facts. Streets ain't what they used to be."

Torrey looked down. "I hear you… just sayin'. Not all of us got safety nets."

They turned back to the game.

Slim vs. Ugh. $500 a game.

Slim chalked his cue. Focused.

Slim: "Bank shot. Side pocket. Watch this."

He lined it. Smooth stroke. Missed by half an inch.

Ugh (grinning): "Gimme that."

Ugh stepped up. One bounce. Banked clean.

Ugh: "That's a game. Run me that five."

Slim laughed. "You better cash app me a rematch."

They say dry wire means you are off the radar.

But in the feds' playbook, silence ain't surrender.

It's surveillance.

You can dodge a raid, duck a plug, lay low in luxury…

But when you've already been written into the indictment—
The only thing you choose is **how fast your freedom fades**.

And tonight?

The dice ain't just rollin' on the pool table.

They rollin' on Slim's life.

CHAPTER 13

Glitter Ain't Gold

Everything that shines doesn't mean it's real.
Just 'cause the water is blue doesn't mean it's deep.
Just 'cause the diamonds dance doesn't mean the foundation is solid.

Because in this world, glitter gets you watched.
Glitter gets you set up.
Glitter gets you *got.*

And just when you think you finally made it out clean—life throws a flashbulb in your face, and reminds you…

That glow you love?
Could be the light before the fall.

📍 MIAMI, FLORIDA – ONE MONTH BEFORE JAY'S ARREST

The air was still thick with salt, sweat, and money.

The **50th birthday yacht party** had been a two-day blur of champagne waterfalls, ocean views, chef-prepped lobster tails, jet skis, and topless dancers painted in gold leaf. Laughter echoed over the water. Stories were born that would live in whispers.

Now it was morning. The sun is hot and unforgiving.

Jay and **Slim** stood on the edge of the marina, duffle bags in hand, waiting on their Uber to the airport.

Jay wore all black—crispy linen, quiet wealth. Slim rocked designer slides, shorts, and a shirt half-buttoned, chain swinging. They were calm. Relaxed. At peace, or so it seemed.

From behind them, **Carlos Alvarez** strolled up in designer shades and a Cuban-link chain heavy as consequence.

Carlos: "Fellas. Appreciate y'all comin' out. Ain't no party without the A."

Jay (smirking): "You did it big. Real talk."

Carlos: "Look... I know we said we were out, but I gotta say— the distro beggin' me to come back. They talkin' big numbers. Real product. Real fast flip."

Jay: "Low... we beat the game. You buildin' a whole subdivision. I'm sittin' on a clean real estate portfolio. My studio poppin'. DG getting spins."

Slim: "I'm 'bout to open my fourth washhouse. Moms finally launched that soul food spot. We up."

Carlos nodded, then leaned in.

Carlos: "I know. I know. I'm good, too. But... man. Ten, maybe twenty mil—*fast.* Head-spinnin' fast. I ain't sayin' I *need* it... but tax-free money?"

Jay (chuckling): "Ain't nothin' tax-free, my boy. Everything comes with a cost. I'm followin' my first mind. I'll see y'all at Slim's wedding."

An **Uber SUV** pulled up, tires crunching the gravel.

Carlos: "Respect. Just think about it."

Jay and Slim tossed their bags in the back and slid in.

📍 ACROSS THE STREET – BLACK SUV – DEA SURVEILLANCE

Inside an unmarked SUV, two **DEA agents** sat in the heat. One adjusted a zoom lens, the other tapped notes into a tablet.

Agent Kent: "Just when we thought we'd lost this case…"

Agent Mendez: "They gave us a gift."

Kent (smirking): "First time we got all three of them together. Slim. Jay. Carlos. That's the opening scene."

Mendez: "Now we can sell the *story.*"

They looked at each other and chuckled.

Kent: "Yacht party was super dope though. Word is the seafood tower came with three waitresses naked underneath."

Mendez: "Don't forget the DJ… or the photos of Carlos and Jay drinkin' together on the upper deck."

Kent: "But that moment? The three of them in the same damn frame? *Priceless.*"

They both laughed, unaware—or fully aware—of just how cruel their patience had been.

📍 INSIDE THE UBER – HEADED TO AIRPORT

Jay stared out the window. Slim scrolled through his phone, but something in the air shifted.

Slim: "You ever miss it?"

Jay glanced over. "Miss what?"

Slim: "The game. That feeling. Like… I ain't gon' lie—it made me feel alive. Back then, every day had a purpose. Danger had flavor."

Jay didn't answer right away.

Jay: "I do miss it sometimes. But then I remember… We were inches from the pen. I was sleepin' with my sneakers on. Couldn't dream right 'cause I kept thinkin' I heard sirens."

Slim nodded. "That truck gettin' pulled in Augusta... that was God's warning."

Jay rubbed his chin. "Yeah. And I ain't tryna make Him say it twice."

Everything glitter ain't gold.

Some of it's bait.

Some of it's a bullet you ain't seen yet.

And sometimes, the celebration?

That's just the setup.

The calm before the doors crash in.

The last good memory before they tell the jury what they want to believe.

Jay thought he made it out.

Slim thought he bought peace.

Carlos thought he could flirt with fire and stay cool.

But the DEA already had the match.

CHAPTER 14

Built from Memory

Life ain't about money.
Ain't about flex.
Ain't even about survival.

It's about **memories**.

Moments that burn themselves into your spirit.

The smell of home.

The sound of your name said with love.

The kind of laugh that makes you forget the weight on your chest.

Some people chase power.
Others chase peace.

But when it's all said and done, the only thing that outlives you... is **what they remember**.

📍 **TAMPA, FLORIDA – SLIM & SIERRA'S HOME – 2 DAYS BEFORE THE WEDDING**

The living room echoed with **NBA 2K banter**.

The boys—**Jalen** and **KJ**,—were locked in a heated game. Controllers clicking, snack wrappers everywhere.

Slim sat on the couch with Sierra, arm draped around her, TV glow dancing on both their faces.

Slim (grinning): "Boys said I gotta be at the bachelor party by 10. Ain't tryin' to be late. They treatin' it like the Super Bowl."

Sierra (laughing): "Well, I'm meeting the girls around 9. Pole lessons and all."

Slim turned toward her, kissed her cheek.

"We really here, huh? Won't be seein' you again till you walkin' down that aisle."

Sierra smiled softly. "I'm so ready. Tired of being the oddball in the house with a different last name. Can't wait for the name— **Mrs. Willis**."

Slim: "Well... forty-eight hours away. Then it's forever."

Sierra reached over, squeezed his hand.

"Drake... I love you. I really do."

Slim (locking eyes): "I love you more. You saved me from a world I wasn't even done with."

They leaned back, letting the quiet wrap around them.

Slim: "The restaurant's comin' together smooth. And the two new washhouse spots? Solid locations. Clean zoning. We're gonna double up before summer."

Sierra: "And after Europe? I wanna start lookin' at that vineyard dream."

Slim: "Best move I ever made? Getting out the game. No lie."

📍 DOWNTOWN – GIRLS' NIGHT – 9:42PM

LED lights glowed in pink and purple inside the Velvet **Whisper Lounge**. Hookahs smoked like incense. A long **snack table** had charcuterie, wings, fruit trays, and mixed drinks at the far end.

Music bumped. Laughter filled the air.

Sierra stood in heels and a one-shoulder jumpsuit, watching the pole instructor demonstrate a slow body roll into a spin.

Instructor (grinning): "Master this… and your man won't even want to leave the house. And when he tips you? Buy yourself a bad bag bitch that money you didn't count for."

The girls roared with laughter.

Tasha (Sierra's best friend): "Girl… teach me. I'm tryna catch the bouquet and a man."

Lexie: "I'm just here to keep you from falling and breaking something!"

Sierra stepped up, gripped the pole, and tried the move.

Not graceful—but determined.

Lexie: "Damn. They really *do* be workin' for that money."

Two of the girls got up and started **twerking by the mirror wall**, drinks in hand.

Tasha (watching Sierra): "You look happy, girl. For real. I remember when you ain't trust nobody. Now look at you—*wifed up.*"

Sierra (laughing): "Because I found a real one. Drake's different. He gave me stability and made me feel safe... like *my love mattered.* This life we are building? Ain't perfect. But it's *real.*"

They all raised their glasses. "To Sierra!"

📍 OTHER SIDE OF TOWN – THE BACHELOR PARTY – 10:51PM

Black SUVs, luxury sedans, and muscle cars were **lined up** outside a private mansion in **Tampa Heights**. Inside, lights pulsed red and gold. DJ **E-Lo** spun trap and R&B. The smell of lemon pepper, Hennessy, and cologne laced the air.

Slim, **Rico**, **Bud**, **Torrey**, **Ugh**, **Malik**, and **Shine** were mid-laugh—each in black designer fits, cigars in hand, dominoes clapping, plates full.

Bud (biting wing): "Aye... if the wedding this lit, I might be joining you."

Ugh: "I'm just tryna survive this liquor."

Shine: "Y'all seen that waitress? Looks like she just stepped off IG Live."

Slim, chill in the cut with a glass of 1942, leaned over to Rico.

Slim: "This is what freedom feels like."

Rico: "Facts. But don't lie... you gon' miss the game."

Slim (smirking): "I miss the thrill. Not the paranoia."

They raised glasses.

📍 ACROSS THE STREET – BLACKED-OUT SURVEILLANCE VAN – 11:07PM

Inside a mobile unit, **Agent Mendez**, **Agent Kent**, and two others sat watching **live feeds**.

Infrared cams showed every vehicle, thermal signatures showed party heat.

Kent: "So what time do we crash the party?"

Mendez: "Let him have a few hours. ... ."

One of the newer agents, **Ramos**, leaned forward, watching.

Ramos: "Man... I couldn't live like that. Being a street dude? No control. Every step feels like a landmine."

Mendez smirked. "That's 'cause it is."

She pointed to the screen.

"Look at him. Laughin'. Dancin'. Toastin'. No idea the next drink might be his last as a free man."

Ten **black cars lined up** two blocks down. Engines running. Vests ready. Paperwork signed.

They built memories.

Shared love.

Made promises with pure hearts.

But fate doesn't ask if you're ready.

And freedom doesn't care if you've changed.

And as Slim laughed with his brothers...as Sierra spun on a pole laughing with her sisters...

The system had already written the ending.

Not with bullets.

But with **binders**.

Witnesses.
And a **clock** about to run out.

The memory they were making tonight?

Would be the last before everything changed.

CHAPTER 15

Laugh Now, Cry Later

They say laugh now… cry later.
But they never say **how fast** later comes.

One minute, you ridin' waves of joy.
Heart full. Room lit.
The future is wide open like the sky on a clear night.

And then—the door crashes in.
The light flips off.
The laughter echoes… and vanishes.

And that's when it hits you:

Everything you thought was solid can be stripped in **seconds**.

🔎 TAMPA HEIGHTS – PRIVATE MANSION – BACHELOR PARTY – 12:34 AM

Slim leaned back in a plush armchair, Hennessy in one hand, cigar in the other. A **lap dancer** sat on him, brown skin glowing under LED lights, whispering sweet lies in his ear.

Beside him, two more women did **pole tricks**, one balancing upside down on one hand, another **blowing fire from her mouth—then from her bare cheeks**, setting the room into wild laughter and applause.

It was everything last night was supposed to be.

Rico, tipsy and smiling, stumbled over with a drink in hand.

Rico (laughing): "Yo, I know I'm lit, but listen… I gotta say this."

Slim raised a brow.

"Appreciate you, bro. Like... for real. You showed me how to stack, how to flip, how to trust the process. You trusted me to be your other set of eyes. That ain't small."

Slim clapped his hand around Rico's neck and pulled him close.

Slim: "You earned that. I didn't give you shit but opportunity. You made it mean somethin'. Now don't get soft on me—ain't the time to start cryin' and confessin'."

They both laughed.

Rico: "Naw, for real. I'm just happy. Happy for you. You are about to marry a queen. You grown-man-in this shit. And we're out here celebratin' right."

Bud climbed on a chair, holding his drink high.

Bud: "Aight! Everybody! Drinks in the air!"

The music dipped. A few dancers paused mid-move. Everyone grabbed a cup.

Bud: "To a real one. Slim, my guy. You have ten toes, from hustle to honor. You ain't just flipped paper—you flipped your *path*. I saw you transform. From trappin' to buildin'. From dodgin' to lovin'. You are an example of what survival looks like when it evolves."

Laughter. Cheers. Applause.

Rico (grinning): "Now that was beautiful, nigga. Damn. I shoulda brought tissues."

The **DJ** grabbed the mic.

DJ E-Lo: "Yooooo—make some noise for my dawg Slim! Next time we see him, he's gon' be a husband!"

The crowd roared.

"Congratulations, king!"

Slim raised his glass. Smiled.

He never saw the **lights flash** outside.

🔎 12:44 AM – FRONT DOORS EXPLODE

BOOM!
BOOM!

The mansion's double doors shattered inward.

Flashbangs. Red laser dots. Screams. Boots. Guns. Chaos.

Men in full tactical gear—DEA, FBI, U.S. Marshals—all screaming commands.

"DOWN! DOWN! HANDS ON THE FLOOR!"

"FEDERAL RAID! DON'T MOVE!"

People hit the ground. Dancers screamed. Bottles crashed.

Slim froze—just a second—before two agents tackled him, twisted his arms, and slammed him chest-down.

"Drake Wills, aka Slim—you're under federal indictment for conspiracy to traffic controlled substances, money laundering, and wire fraud."

One agent held up a **printed warrant** with his name in bold black ink.

Agent Mendez: "You have the right to remain silent..."

Slim didn't hear the rest. His ears rang.

They dragged him toward the door, barefoot, shirt ripped, surrounded by blinding camera flashes from body cams.

Rico and Bud stood in shock.

Rico: "What in the *hell* just happened?!"

Bud (whispering): "They got him…"

Rico (shaking): "What do we tell Sierra?"

Time froze.

📍 DOWNTOWN TAMPA – VELVET WHISPER LOUNGE – SAME TIME

Music blasted. *Future's "March Madness"* turned the room into a dream-state—dancers on poles, bottles with sparklers, hookah clouds heavy in the air.

Sierra was laughing with **Tasha** and **Lexie**, cheeks red from champagne.

Her phone lit up.

She blinked. "Why Rico callin' me right now?"

She stepped away, still smiling, phone to her ear.

Sierra: "Rico… what's up? You at the party?"

The voice on the other end wasn't loud or excited.

It was… broken.

Rico: "They got him."

Sierra: "Got *who*?"

Rico (choked): "The feds. They just picked up Drake."

Her whole face changed. Smile gone. Eyes frozen. Glass is still in hand, but her body is no longer moving.

Sierra (barely whispering): "For what?"

Rico: "happened so fast I can't remember what they said. Just handed him the warrant and dipped."

Sierra dropped the phone to her side.

Everyone noticed.

The music faded. Even the DJ noticed her stillness.

Tasha ran over.

Tasha: "Girl? What happened?!"

Sierra's knees buckled slightly. Tasha and Lexie grabbed her.

The dancers slowed. One girl got off the pole mid-move. Bartenders turned down the volume. The room dimmed from celebration into confusion.

Sierra (whispering): "They took him."

Lexie: "Who?!"

Sierra: "The feds... they took Drake..."

Silence.

The music stopped completely.

Everyone stood still—one moment away from celebration...and now stuck inside heartbreak.

Laugh now...

Cry later.

But nobody told them the laughs would be recorded.

The champagne spilled.

The kisses at midnight were replaced with cuffs at the door.

And now?

All the memories they tried to build...

Are being used as proof that they never left their life behind.

CHAPTER 16

When Reality Sinks In

When the smoke clears, and the doors are closed,
when the celebration's over and the cuffs bite your skin—

That's when *reality* walks in.

Not loud.
Not fast.
But heavy.

It sits on your chest like a weight you can't push off.
And at that moment... you finally understand.

🔎 PRESENT DAY – THREE DAYS SINCE THE ARRESTS

Jay sat in a federal holding cell in Atlanta, across from his defense attorney. The room was pale, fluorescent, and smelled like cold coffee and stale carpet. His hands were cuffed to a metal loop on the table.

The lawyer laid out a few papers. No smile. No fluff.

Attorney Marshall: "The official charges are in. Federal conspiracy—relevant conduct attached. Money laundering. And they're pinning you with a leadership role over five or more individuals."

Jay leaned back, expression still. His mind started calculating.

Jay: "What's the time frame?"

Marshall: "2013 to 2016."

Jay's eyebrows furrowed.

Jay: "I've been clean since 2014... I know what I walked away from. That's ten years ago, man."

Marshall: "That's not how conspiracy law works. If they can prove the *network* still benefited from groundwork you laid, they'll make you wear the whole jacket. Relevant conduct covers all activity connected to the conspiracy, whether you were still hands-on or not."

Jay exhaled—slow, long. A silence blanketed the room.

Jay (softly): "You think I can get a bond?"

The attorney paused, folding his hands.

Marshall: "Doubt it. You flagged high risk, plus they labeled you leadership. But I'm gonna push for it. We'll file for a bond hearing. Could take a few weeks."

Jay looked down at his shackled wrists. Everything in him wanted to scream. But all he did... was nod.

Marshall: "Jay... you're lookin' at thirty to life. That's what they bringing to the table."

That sentence sucked the air out of the room.
 Like someone just cracked the seal on a coffin.

Jay didn't blink. Didn't cry. But his soul bent under the weight.

📍 NORTH ATLANTA – OB-GYN OFFICE – SAME DAY

Princess sat on the edge of the exam table, her hands rubbing gently over her lower belly. Her voice was soft.

Princess: "I saw red in my underwear. Just a small spot."

The **doctor** asked a few questions, ran the ultrasound, and took some samples.

Doctor Lewis: "I'm not seeing anything critical. But I'd say stress is definitely a factor. Your vitals are a little elevated. I want you to rest. No sudden movements. Hydrate. Let's give your body what it needs to protect the baby."

Princess nodded. Swallowed her fear.

Outside the office, she walked slowly, her mother by her side.

Ms. Green: "Everything okay?"

Princess hesitated. Then nodded.

Princess: "They said it's stress. I just need to rest."

Ms. Green (softly): "That's what I'm here for. You focus on carrying that baby. We gon' get through this. Don't let fear trick you into forgetting who you are. You still have a future."

They hugged in silence.

📍 TALLAHASSEE FEDERAL DETENTION CENTER – MORNING MOVEMENT

Drake sat on the bottom bunk, lacing his shoes up as the **CO** handed him the official transfer slip.

CO: "Pack up. The bus leaves in an hour. You're headed to Atlanta. Case outta Northern District."

He nodded, stood up, and started folding his things into a mesh bag. Back in the room, **Craig**—his cellmate, older, gray at the beard—watched from across the room.

Craig: "You headed to ATL?"

Drake: "Yeah. Just told me."

Craig: "You must be tied to somethin' big. They don't move you that far unless they settin' the table."

Drake looked at him, eyes weary.

Drake: "They hit me with charges from years ago. I swear to God I was clean. Got a restaurant. Real estate. I changed my whole life."

Craig: "You ain't the first, won't be the last. When feds want a win, they grab *everyone* who ever breathed the same air. I bet they ran three, four grand juries before they came for you."

Drake: "As far as I know, I'm the only one they picked up."

Craig: "We'll see once you hit that ATL tank. You never know who is already flippin' or singin' behind closed doors."

Drake didn't respond.

He stared at the chipped paint on the wall.

📍 SIERRA'S APARTMENT – EVENING

Sierra sat on the floor of her bedroom, still in her robe. Her phone was in her hand, but the screen was blank.

She hadn't eaten. The wedding dress was hanging on the closet door.
White. Untouched. A symbol of something now postponed... or lost.

Sierra (to herself): "We were supposed to be married right now... We were supposed to be in Santorini."

Her best friend **Tasha** sat beside her.

Tasha: "You said he was clean, right? That has to mean something. This ain't over."

Sierra: "But we don't know *anything*. No court date. No explanation. Just... gone."

She put the phone to her chest, wishing it would ring.

It didn't.

When reality sinks in, you stop living in the illusion of your intentions and start drowning in the results of your associations.

Jay, Drake, and their families weren't guilty by action...they were guilty by design.

A web woven years ago is still sticky enough to hold them now.

And as the clock ticks louder, the only thing left to do... is pray you make it out before it fully wraps around your throat.

CHAPTER 17

"Mind Games & Shackles"

The locks never get comfortable.

The cuffs cut tighter the more you try to adjust.

And the more you squirm, the more you realize—you did this to yourself.

There's no worse silence than the one inside your own head when your ankles clink with every step, your wrists burn from steel, and the ride is long enough for regret to speak louder than pride.

📍 U.S. MARSHAL BUS TRANSFER – FLORIDA TO GEORGIA

Drake sat in the middle of a diesel-powered transport bus headed for Atlanta, flanked by a hundred other men in khaki jumpsuits, shackled at the hands and feet, double-looped in chains that connected waist to ankles. The air inside was thick—no A/C, no open windows, just the engine rumbling and the stench of tension, sweat, and sorrow.

The **holding tank earlier that morning** had been stacked with bodies like a warzone refugee center—men packed shoulder to shoulder, pacing or sitting cross-legged, mumbling prayers or staring off into nothing. Some played tough. Others cried in silence. No one wanted to talk about their charges... but everyone listened when someone else did.

In federal holding, it's not always what you *say* that matters— It's what you *don't* say that tells the most.

Now on the bus, each name was called by **groups of three**, processed, cuffed, and loaded like cargo. No eye contact with marshals. No questions. Just **roll call and steel**.

Drake had been quiet most of the ride. His eyes scanned the other passengers—some laughing too loud, some dozing, some talking about time like it was poker chips.

In front of him, two older inmates were talking through the heavy chain belts around their waists.

Inmate 1 (gritty voice): "They gave me 180 months for my girl's damn pistol. Her house. Her name. Gun in her drawer."

Inmate 2 (shocked): "She didn't claim it?"

Inmate 1: "She did! Still hit me with possession. Said my two priors made it a wrap. Called it 'Armed Career Criminal Act'—ACC. Mandatory fifteen."

Inmate 2: "Damn... feds don't play fair."

Inmate 1 (laughs bitterly): "Fair? Ain't no *fair* in the federal court. There's just enhancements and mandatory minimums."

Across from them, another convo popped off.

Inmate 3 (light-skinned, late 30s): "I was lookin' at five flat, ended up with 135 months. Said I had a *stash location*, two runners, and they hit me for *use of a communication facility*—because of some damn phone calls."

Inmate 4: "Ain't the charge, homie. It's your *history*. That guideline sheet? That enhancement page? That's the real trap."

Drake listened close. Eyes half-shut. Head leaned back.

The mind games begin long before court.

They start in the echoes of stories like these.

They make you question *what they really got*, and *what they just want you to believe they got*.

His eyes closed as he muttered a short prayer under his breath.

Drake (softly): "God, just walk with me. I don't know what's coming, but don't let it break me…"

Suddenly, the sound of **gagging** broke the mood. Heads turned.

One of the inmates had used the **portable toilet** in the back of the bus.

Inmate 5 (groaning): "Yo, guard… somebody *gotta* crack a window. Man shittin' out his soul back there."

Inmate 6 (laughing): "You shoulda left that milk alone, boy! That gas hittin' like a conspiracy charge."

Laughter rippled through the rows.

Inmate 5 (still moaning): "This is *cruel and unusual punishment.* I smell death."

Even the **marshal** cracked a smile but said nothing, just reached up and turned the **radio volume** up.

Soon, **Young Thug and Rich Homie Quan's "Lifestyle"** blasted through the busted speakers. A handful of the younger inmates started rapping along, loud and off-key.

"I did a lot of shit just to live this here lifestyle…"

The chorus dropped and nearly the whole bus joined in—rapping, bouncing in their seats, some with their eyes closed like it was 2014 again.

Drake didn't join in.

He just stared out the reinforced window, watching the trees and cars pass.

That song used to be the soundtrack to his life.

Now it was the irony of it.

Money. Fame. Fast cars. Dirty deals.

All bought on the back of bad decisions.

And now he'd give *everything* just to roll the window down,

feel the wind hit his face, and drive *his own* damn car again.

The man next to him turned, extending a cuffed hand.

JD (smirking): "Name's JD. Outta Miami. You?"

Drake: "Drake. Atlanta. Raised in Tampa."

JD: "What did they get you on?"

Drake: "They say conspiracy... but I don't even know what evidence they got yet."

JD: "Shit, I'm down on *ice*. Gave me 120 for two ounces. No guns, no violence. Just said I fit the profile. Called it 'drug trafficking with enhancement for aggravating role.' I was my *own* codefendant."

Drake nodded slowly. JD's story hit too close.

JD: "They don't need to catch you doin' it, bro. They just need to make it *look* like you could've done it. Paint the picture, let the jury connect the dots."

Drake: "That's the part that messes with you. You start replayin' every phone call, every person you dealt with. Wonderin' what they *really* real or what."

JD (leaning back): "Ain't no worse jail than your own thoughts."

The bus rolled on toward Atlanta.

Chains rattled.

Feet shifted.

But for Drake, time stood still.

He didn't see buildings.

He didn't hear lyrics.

All he saw was Sierra's face... and her wedding dress still hanging untouched.
All he felt was the weight of not knowing how long it would be before he could feel *free* again.

They don't just chain your hands.

They chain your memory...your guilt...your hope.

The federal system doesn't rush to convict.

They wait.

They *watch*.

And when they come... they already convinced the jury.

The real sentence starts not when the gavel drops—but when you can no longer tell if you're innocent...or just unlucky.

CHAPTER 18

"Was It Worth It?"

Each day behind bars chips away at the illusion of invincibility.

The lights, the money, the luxury cars, the jewelry—all of it fades.

Every drip of time makes you wish you had sat longer with the ones who *actually cared.*

Because here, the noise quiets.

And what echoes loudest is one question:

Was it worth it?

📍 ATLANTA FEDERAL DETENTION CENTER – MORNING

Jay stepped out of his cell as the metal door slammed behind him.
The corridor reeked of ammonia, old sweat, and regret.

Orange lights buzzed overhead.

Guards stood like stone statues—expressionless, mechanical, indifferent.

He moved toward the **chow hall**, stepping over a trail of roaches near the wall.

To his left, a row of inmates in **red jumpsuits**—segregation tier.

Eyes blank. Mouths sealed. Some rocking slowly in their seats.

Jay always hated the sight.

It was a reminder of how far one could fall, and how fast.

The **mess line** moved like clockwork:

10 minutes to eat, **5 minutes to move**, **15-minute showers**, a race to shit in private while your cellmate walked the tier, **and maybe**—if you were lucky—get clean boxers that fit.

Jay grabbed his tray. Watery eggs. Burnt toast. Half-ripe banana. He scanned the room until a familiar face stopped him mid-step.

Drake.

Sitting at the far end of the table, head low, fork in hand.

Jay walked over.

Jay: "Bro… no way. They got you too?"

Drake stood up fast and wrapped his arms around him.

Drake: "Man… at my *bachelor party*. The day before the wedding, bro. They play dirty."

Jay (exhaling): "That's wild. I thought this was from some guy I sold to outta Atlanta, but now? Man, I don't know."

Drake: "You heard from Carlos? Have they touched him yet?"

Jay: "Not yet. But time always tells. My lawyer said I'm facing **30 to life** off the top."

Drake froze.

Drake: "Damn. That deep?"

Jay: "Yeah… and we ain't even seen the discovery yet. They talk about *conspiracy*, *money laundering*, *leadership roles*, *and continuing criminal enterprise*. Everything under the sun."

Drake shook his head, eyes scanning the bleak space around them.

Drake: "How the hell the phones work here?"

Jay: "It's hell, bro. Place crawling with rats. Roaches big as baby turtles. You gotta pay a dude five stacks just to get a line that ain't cuttin' off every three minutes."

He pointed across the chow hall.

Jay (cont'd): "That's the phone line. The line stay packed. The shower looks like it hasn't been cleaned since Bush was president. Have you seen Atlanta on the news? They weren't lyin'. Worst transit in the Bureau."

Drake rubbed his face and sighed.

Drake: "Man... I heard that on the bus. Though they were exaggeratin'. But this shit... this real."

Before either could say more, a correctional officer walked up with a clipboard.

CO: "Jay Willis. Drake Brooks. Suit up. You got court. Van's waiting."

They looked at each other. Then down at their trays.

The food suddenly didn't matter.

📍 FEDERAL COURTHOUSE – ATLANTA

The courtroom was cold, sterile, and echoing with whispers.

Princess, Sierra, and a few close relatives sat in the gallery.

Eyes red. Hands clenched.

When Jay and Drake were led in, dressed in beige jumpsuits and shackles, the women stood instinctively.

A lump swelled in Princess' throat.

Sierra's lip trembled.

Jay's lawyer leaned toward him.

Lawyer (low voice): "They're gonna hit you with the charges first. Don't react. Stay composed."

Jay gave a tight nod.

The clerk stood.

Clerk: "In the matter of United States vs. Jason Collins — charges include:
Conspiracy to distribute controlled substances,
Money Laundering,
Leadership role involving five or more individuals, and
Continuing Criminal Enterprise under 848."

Princess gasped. She clutched her stomach.

Judge: "Mr. Collins, these charges carry a statutory minimum of 30 years to life in federal prison."

His mother covered her mouth.

His uncle shook his head.

Princess nearly fainted. **Jay's brother** caught her before she hit the ground.

AUSA: "Your Honor, due to the severity of these charges and the scope of the ongoing investigation, we request **no bond** be granted."

Jay's lawyer stood, calm but assertive.

Lawyer: "Your Honor, my client has no recent criminal history. He has deep ties to the community, including property holdings. We're willing to put up real estate, monitored release, or any reasonable conditions the Court deems necessary. He is not a flight risk."

The judge shook his head slowly.

Judge: "This Court finds that the nature of the charges, including the leadership role and historical pattern, justify detention pending trial. **Bond denied.**"

Jay didn't flinch.

He looked back at Princess, saw the tears fall, but didn't blink. He just nodded once. Silently telling her, *hold on.*

Next came **Drake**.

Same charges.
Same denial.
Same heartbreak.

📍 COURTHOUSE HALLWAY – AFTER COURT

Princess stormed out of the courtroom, breathing fast. Her mother walked beside her, holding her elbow.

Jay's lawyer approached.

Princess: "Tell me the truth… is he really facing *thirty to life?*"

Lawyer: "Right now? Yes. That's what the charges carry. But I haven't seen the full discovery yet. We'll know more in a few weeks."

Princess wobbled again.

Jay's brother caught her shoulder.

Princess (teary): "How much more money do you need?"

Lawyer: "At least **eighty thousand** to fight it properly. Expert witnesses, motions, travel. If we're going to trial… we need every edge."

Princess nodded slowly, wiped her face, and exhaled like the weight of the world was on her back.

Outside the courthouse, **Sierra** stood on the steps.

Princess: "You can stay with me if you want. Till this trial is over."

Sierra (softly): "Thank you. I'm staying with my sister for now… but let's definitely meet up. I don't wanna do this alone."

They hugged each other tightly—no words left.

In the background, camera shutters clicked.

Reporters stood on the edge of the courthouse steps like vultures.

But for the women left behind, there was no media angle.

Just pain.

And questions.

And the empty space where a wedding was supposed to be.

They thought they beat the game.

Built legit businesses. Bought houses. Planned weddings.

But the feds never move quickly.

They let the clock tick.

They let you *celebrate*.

Then they come like a thief in the night—and turn your memories into **evidence**.

CHAPTER 19

"The Ghost of Ghosts"
It's always the ones you think are real who hide the deepest lies.
And money?
Money blinds.
Money distracts.
Money is the perfect camouflage to keep you from seeing the truth…until it's too late.

SIX MONTHS EARLIER – ATLANTA, GEORGIA – DEA FIELD OFFICE

The fluorescent lights hummed overhead. Papers stacked high. A whiteboard cluttered with surveillance photos, names, arrows, cash trails, and an ominous name circled twice in red ink: **Carlos Ramirez.**

Agent **Nina Calderon** leaned against the wall, arms crossed. Agent **Mitch Donovan** flipped through the folder in front of him.

Across the table sat **Jorge Medina**, sharp fade, designer shades resting on his collar, his knee bouncing with tension.

Donovan: "How can you help *us* help *you*, Jorge?"

Jorge leaned in, calm but focused.

Jorge: "I can get y'all Carlos Ramirez."

Calderon chuckled.

Calderon: "Impossible. He's been cold for two years. Ghosted everyone. We've been tracking this man since '08—never left a fingerprint."

Jorge (smirking): "He's got problems. Big ones. Builders ran off with his money. Lost six figures. He's vulnerable. We talked a few weeks back."

Donovan and Calderon exchanged a glance.

Calderon: "Name your play."

Jorge: "Bait. I dangle the right order—make it look like it'll fix his problem and disappear. He'll bite."

Donovan scratched his chin.

Donovan: "You really think you can pull in the ghost of ghosts?"

Jorge (grinning): "Trust me."

🔎 EAST ATLANTA – HOME DEPOT PARKING LOT

Carlos Ramirez and his wife **Leticia** walked hand in hand, carts full of tile samples and hardware.

Leticia: "How much longer do you think before the house is finished?"

Carlos exhaled, glanced down at his receipt.

Carlos: "Couple more months. You know how construction goes—delays, rain, lazy workers…"

Leticia: "Well, the lawn service is holding. Plus *Maritza* turns eighteen in three weeks. She wants a Benz and a graduation trip to Costa Rica. We have stay true to our word Carlos."

They reached the SUV. Carlos loaded the trunk, sweat glistening on his brow.

Carlos: "I got it. No problem."

Later that evening, Carlos stood in front of a job site—a concrete shell of a luxury home half-done.
Two workers unloaded beams and cinder blocks.

Carlos: "Y'all pouring the slab tomorrow?"

The **Project Manager**, a scruffy guy in tan boots and a faded Braves hat, gave a short nod.

PM: "Yeah, boss. The first crew botched the layout—set us back weeks. But we're back on track."

Carlos didn't reply. Just stared at the wood frame.

He knew delays cost more than time.
They cost trust.
And money.

🔎 NEXT DAY – DOWNTOWN ATLANTA – MI CASA LATIN BISTRO

A Latin jazz trio played soft in the corner as **Carlos** and **Jorge** sat in a private booth away from the main crowd. Empanadas untouched. Sweat beading on Jorge's glass.

Jorge: "I need **three hundred bricks**."

Carlos blinked, fast.
His mind did the math. Roughly 7.5 million on the street.
But his face stayed neutral.

Carlos: "You know I been out of the game."

Jorge: "I know. But I got two buyers in town. Serious ones. I had the play set up, but my people fumbled the bag. The quality was trash. These guys don't come around twice."

Carlos looked past him toward the kitchen. Waiters moved in rhythm.

Normal life kept flowing—while the underworld came knocking again.

Jorge (lower voice): "Bro… remember when you lost everything? Who helped you rebuild?"

Carlos nodded slowly.

Carlos: "You did."

Jorge: "Exactly. And I never asked for anything back. Till now. This one time, we cleaned up. You already said you could use extra cash. They ain't asking for loyalty—just product. Quick in, quick out."

Carlos wiped his hands, thinking.

Carlos: "Let me make a few calls. I'll hit you tomorrow."

Jorge (smiling): "That's all I ask."

They fist-bumped.

What Carlos didn't know—was that the booth behind him had a planted mic.
And outside, across the street, two unmarked black Tahoes sat watching, windows cracked.

🔎 DEA SURVEILLANCE VAN – LIVE FEED

Agents Calderon and Donovan sat listening to the audio as Jorge walked out.

Donovan smirked.

Donovan: "He bit. I knew it."

Calderon leaned back, arms folded.

Calderon: "Three hundred bricks? This ain't street hustle. This is cartel volume."

The sound of laughter came from the agents in the back.

Junior Agent Boyd: "That's our ticket. We finally gonna nail Ramirez. The press is gonna love this."

Donovan: "We just went from maybe to major. When those bricks show up—we don't just have a case. We got a *story.*"

Calderon: "Get the wire. Get the photo log. Get him driving to the meeting. We want everything."

Boyd grinned.

Boyd: "We're about to catch the ghost of ghosts."

They raised their coffee cups and toasted the coming storm.

Carlos thought he was solving a problem.

What he didn't realize—

was that he'd just walked into the jaws of history.

The setup was clean.

The bait was perfect.

And the men behind the curtain had all the time in the world.

Because in the game of power…

The truth is never what it seems.

CHAPTER 20

"False Moves, Real Time"

The thing about the game is, you can only control *your* moves.

It doesn't matter how perfect you play—someone else's mistake…their false move…can cost you everything.

Your name.

Your freedom.

Sometimes—your life.

🔎 SIX MONTHS EARLIER – EAST ATLANTA – RAMIREZ HOME

Carlos Ramirez sat on the edge of the bed, lacing up his sneakers with the kind of speed that hinted at nerves.

In the kitchen, **Leticia Ramirez** stirred café con leche. Their daughter, **Maritza**, played TikTok videos aloud on her phone, sprawled on the couch.

Carlos: "I got a one-time play. Clean. I don't even touch nothin'. Just connect the dots."

Leticia paused, turned slowly.

Leticia: "What kind of play?"

Carlos (quietly): "Half a million. One move. Done in a week."

Leticia: "That ain't an answer. What kind of *play*?"

Carlos walked into the kitchen, keeping his voice low.

Carlos: "I connect the supplier with the buyers. I just bridge it. That's it. No hands, no risk."

Leticia placed her spoon down, folded her arms.

Leticia: "You've been out. Almost for years. We said no more. You're building houses now. You run a business. Why go back?"

Carlos: "Because the business *pays the bills*. Barely. That's all it does. I need new money, *real* money."

Leticia: "Who's it with?"

Carlos hesitated.

Carlos: "Jorge."

Leticia's eyes sharpened.

Leticia: "Mmm. I told you. That man didn't sit right with me. Snake energy. Flashy mouth. Never had clean eyes."

Carlos waved it off.

Carlos: "It's one time. One favor. 500K and I'm done. I promise, Letty. Just trust me."

Leticia didn't argue. But her silence was a warning louder than words.

📍 NORTH ATLANTA PARK – LITTLE LEAGUE DIAMOND

Cheers exploded from the stands as **Jay Willoughby**'s team sealed the final out.

Jay—white tee, team cap backward—slapped hands with the players, smiling wide.

Jay: "That's what I'm talking about! That's how you close a game! But listen—we are not done. Next team? They are beasts. Bigger. Faster. But they ain't got *heart* like y'all."

The boys huddled close, sweaty and beaming.

Jay (grinning): "Y'all we have one day to get ready.?"

Parents clapped nearby. **Coach Love**, Jay's assistant coach, stepped over with his clipboard.

Love: "That lefty on the next team? Throws gas. We'll need Malik or Corey starting. Can't afford errors."

Jay nodded.

Jay: "Let's rotate Corey at third. Put D.J. at short. I trust his glove."

As they strategized, **Princess** walked over with two hot dogs and a bottle of water.

Princess (smiling): "The game was fire today. Boys were locked in."

Jay kissed her on the cheek.

Jay: "One more win and we are in the finals. They remember Coach Jay's team for years."

Princess laughed.

Princess: "Let's go check that other game. See if next week lookin' light or scary."

📍 WEST MIDTOWN – LUXE EVENTS HALL

Sierra twirled slowly in the grand ballroom, beaming. Crystal chandeliers. White marble floors. She clutched a swatch of fabric in one hand.

Sierra: "This is *perfect*. Baby, it's everything I pictured."

Slim stood with arms crossed, nodding with a half-smile.

Slim: "As long as you are happy, I'm good."

Wedding Planner (Cassandra Brooks): "The DJ booth goes here. Full bar setup on the back wall. You want hookahs, yes?"

Sierra: "Yes, but classy. Gold-stemmed ones. No plastic hoses."

Slim: "Where are the food tables?"

Cassandra: "We'll have a buffet line over there, plated service for the head table."

Slim rubbed his temples, overwhelmed.

Slim (muttering): "Just ready to get this part over with…"

Sierra: "Don't play. You know you can't wait to see me walk that aisle."

He smirked.

Slim: "Aight, you right."

📍 DEA – ATLANTA FIELD OFFICE – SURVEILLANCE OPERATIONS BRIEFING ROOM

Agents Nina Calderon, Mitch Donovan, and **Terrence Banks** stood over a wide conference table. On the digital screen behind them: a map of Georgia. Pins. Routes. Faces.

Calderon: "We got confirmation from Jorge. Carlos is engaged in a 300-kilo transaction. Street value? North of 7 mil."

Donovan: "That's our open door."

Banks: "What about Jay and Slim?"

Calderon clicked the remote, switching screens. Photos of Jay coaching, Slim at the event venue.

Calderon: "No active involvement—yet. But we believe they're still connected. Based on wire intercepts and history, this entire circle functions as a rotating enterprise."

Donovan: "Carlos and Jay keeping it clean invested in the music business, real estate, and wash houses. They break, time our best friend."

Banks: "You think we got enough to tie them together legally?"

Calderon: "No. Not yet. But this play with Carlos? It's the start. Operation Three Kings is now *greenlit.*"

Donovan: "Let's build it right. Quiet. No leaks. One mistake and they vanish."

They all nodded.

Calderon: "We take them down when the story's airtight. Big. Beautiful. And bulletproof."

And just like that…the line was cast.

One man's desperation…another man's betrayal…and three lives about to collide in a storm they'd never see coming.

Because in the drug game, you can make all the right moves—

but if the wrong person folds?

You lose the whole board.

CHAPTER 21

"The Favor That Costs Everything"

They say the love of money is the root of all evil.
But money?
Money ain't evil.
It's survival.
It's a house not getting foreclosed.
It's keeping the lights on when the fridge is already empty.
It's tuition.
It's protection.
It's freedom—
Until it becomes a chain.

📍 SOUTH ATLANTA – BACK ROOM, CANTINA VERDE

Dim lights. A red bulb buzzed overhead. Salsa music played low in the distance beyond the door.

Carlos Ramirez sat across from his old connect—**Heffy Morales**—a thick man with rough hands, silver chains, and eyes that never blinked.

Heffy: "So let me get this straight… You out the game for years, only see you at wedding and birthdays. Then show up needin' *three hundred keys*?"

Carlos leaned back, tried to appear calm, but his fingers fidgeted beneath the table.

Carlos: "pretty much you know I'm the rain man. This is a one-time favor. For an old friend. Guy helped me when I had nothin'. I'm just returning the favor."

Heffy cracked his knuckles.

Heffy: "One-time moves? Always turn into three and four. Plus I need you back on the team."

Carlos: "I use this extra tax free cash. Building this subdivision costing more than I calculated."

Heffy studied him. Long pause.

Heffy: "Count the money first. Make sure it's on point. You know how I move."

Carlos: "Of course. I'd never brought you short money neat and clean."

Heffy (grinning): "Let's eat for old time sake."

They shook hands. Carlos didn't smile.

🔎 OUTSIDE CANTINA VERDE – SURVEILLANCE VAN

DEA Agents Nina Calderon and **Mitch Donovan** sat watching through binoculars and parabolic mics.

Calderon: "Has this bar ever come up on our radar before?"

Donovan: "Not to my knowledge. No wire taps. Nothing flagged."

Calderon: "That means it's clean. Could be perfect for post-meet surveillance. Let's log it as a staging point."

Donovan sipped coffee, never taking his eyes off the door.

Donovan: "We take this down clean? We don't just close Three Kings—we get promoted off this shit."

Calderon: "We're still cooking Jorge though, right?"

Donovan: "Oh yeah. This is his third time. And it's gonna be his last."

📍 CARLOS'S MERCEDES – LEAVING THE MEETING

Carlos dialed.

Carlos: "It's green light. But I need to run through the money first. Count it, make sure on point. You know."

On the other end, **Jorge** answered quickly.

Jorge: "No problem. Just say when."

They hung up.

In a nearby car, a DEA tech turned to Calderon.

Tech: "You hear that? They talkin' five million in street money."

Calderon: "Do we even have assets for that kind of cash?"

Donovan: "Doesn't matter. We'll make it happen. Either way—Operation Three Kings just got fuel."

📍 CARLOS'S HOUSE – PHONE CALL

Carlos leaned against the kitchen counter, dialing **Leticia**. She answered while helping their daughter with homework.

Carlos: "Tell Mari to go pick out that Benz. 20K down, we cover the rest next week."

Leticia: "Carlos..."

Carlos: "Don't start. It's done."

He tapped the speaker.

Maritza (screaming): "You the best, Daddy! I love you!!"

Carlos smiled as he ended the call—then looked out the window with eyes that held both pride... and guilt.

📍 JORGE'S APARTMENT – BURNER PHONE CALL

Jorge sat in a dark room, watching TV on mute. His DEA handler answered.

Jorge: "He's in. Needs to count the cash first. It's real."

DEA Handler: "No problem. Let him swim. But keep him close."

📍 NORTH ATLANTA – MUSIC STUDIO

Jay, **Big Cheese**, **Bossman**, and **Hot Rod** sat on a couch, smoke floating upward. Inside the booth, rising artist **DG** flowed hard over a trap beat.

Big Cheese: "He spazzin'. We need to press the gas on this promo run."

Hot Rod: "Franchises outta Macon and Chattanooga got open dates. We hit them small towns, it moves faster."

Bossman: "You talk to Future people about that feature?"

Jay nodded.

Jay: "Yeah. They want 30. But if we pull it right, it'll double what we put in. I say we press."

They nodded in agreement, energized, unaware of the heat rising silently beneath their feet.

📍 EVENT HALL BAKERY LOUNGE –

Slim and **Sierra** sat side-by-side as a server laid out five mini cakes.

Server: "Red velvet, lemon buttercream, classic vanilla, bourbon pecan, and strawberry champagne."

Sierra (biting into red velvet): "Mmm. This one."

Slim (mouth full): "That's fire. I like the bourbon one too though."

Sierra: "You just like the word *bourbon*."

They laughed.

Slim: "This wedding costing more than some folk's houses."

Sierra: "But it's ours. I want this day to be unforgettable."

She paused.

Sierra: "You ever think about another baby?"

Slim (grinning): "We ain't even married yet and you tryna give me gray hairs?"

Sierra: "I'm just saying. You, me, lil girl with your forehead…"

Slim (laughing): "Lord help me."

Every empire falls by one small crack.

Not always from greed.

Sometimes… just a favor owed.

A little pressure.

A little pride.

And by the time you smell smoke,

The fire's already been burning for months.

CHAPTER 22

"The Count Before The Storm"

Nobody wanna do time. Don't let them fool you— Not your favorite hustler. Not your favorite trap queen. "I" comes before "U" in the alphabet for a reason. Self-preservation doesn't wait for loyalty to catch up.

DEA FIELD OFFICE – DOWNTOWN ATLANTA

Inside a small, dimly lit briefing room, Agent Derrick Rowe—tall, sharp suit, no nonsense—stood over Jorge, who looked rattled.

AGENT ROWE You're going with us for the buy. Non-negotiable.

JORGE That wasn't the deal. You said—

AGENT ROWE (cutting him off) I'm saying now. This your third time, Jorge. We run this—not you.

Another agent slid a duffel onto the table—zip cracked open to reveal bundled bricks of money. Rowe slapped the top stack.

AGENT ROWE (CONT'D) This is what you get. One mil. Just enough to make him bite. Once Carlos starts counting, we move.

Jorge, bitter but boxed in, nodded.

JORGE (quietly) He ain't gonna like it.

AGENT ROWE He doesn't have to. Send the text.

WEST END – OUTSIDE CARLOS'S TOWNHOUSE

Carlos Ramirez sat parked in his matte-black Yukon, windows cracked, engine humming low. His voice boomed over the speakers—singing along with "El Rey" by Vicente Fernández.

CARLOS (singing) "Pero sigo siendo el rey!"

Carlos sang it loud, proud. He banged the steering wheel twice, stepped out, adjusted his gold chain, and walked inside.

INSIDE THE TOWNHOUSE

The scent of Pine-Sol and peppermints lingered in the air. A modest two-story setup—tile floors, granite countertops, family pictures with blurred faces on the wall.

His sister—Marisol—was already in place, three money counters buzzing like chainsaws.

"Bro... all three counters ? This gotta be big money play "

"Sometimes you have to remind them who has the juice," Carlos said, already stepping deeper into the living room. "I know I'll pay you twenty-five racks. Like old times"

Marisol glanced over at him, a sly smile curling across her lips. "I haven't seen you this alive in years. Shit... you damn near glowing."

"Haven't felt this good in a long time. It's making my dick hard."

"Gross." She rolled her eyes. "I don't know why you left the game in the first place."

Carlos sighed and leaned on the counter. "America changed me. Nah... some strange shit started happening. It was time for a break."

"Well, I'm out. Leave the money in my room—don't touch my stash."

They hugged like siblings who'd been through things they never put into words. She tossed her bag over her shoulder and walked out.

FIVE MINUTES LATER – FRONT DOOR KNOCKS

Jorge walked in wearing all black. Behind him, a tall, quiet Black man in army cargo gear stepped in, holding a duffel bag.

Carlos 's eyes narrowed. "¿Qué carajos, Jorge? ¿Quién es este tipo?"

"Tranquilo, carnal," Jorge dijo softly. "Es buena gente. Solo es respaldo."

Carlos 's tone cut sharper. "¡Tú no traes a nadie a mi casa sin decirme! ¡Eso es una falta de respeto!"

"Es solo una entrega, hermano. Nada más. Confía."

Carlos stared hard, jaw tight. He didn't like it. But after a beat, he turned to the counter.

"Vamos a contarlo."

They opened the bag—banded stacks of hundreds dumped onto the granite. Machines buzzed. Paper slid fast. Carlos checked the stamps, organized the bundles with veteran fingers.

HALFWAY THROUGH COUNTING

Carlos's phone rang. Heffy's name lit the screen. He stepped away, pressed the speaker.

"How is it looking?" Heffy asked.

"Counting now. We'll need time, but it's clean so far."

"Stay sharp."

Carlos turned sideways, glancing back at Jorge.

Jorge chuckled. "Remember that one time... the 18-wheeler in El Paso?"

"You forgot it was your fuck-up," Carlos replied.

They shared a stiff laugh. The tension between them never really left.

The phone rang again—this time, his daughter.

"Daddy!" she chirped. "I picked out the Benz! Red seats! Pizza in an hour?"

Carlos softened. "Of course, mi reina. Soon as I'm done."

He hung up. Turned back toward the money—

And the walls exploded.

BOOM.

DOOR CRASHES IN. GLASS SHATTERS.

VOICES OVERLAP—

"FEDERAL AGENTS!"

"GET ON THE GROUND!"

"HANDS! DOWN! NOW!"

Red lasers cut through the fog of chaos. Carlos dropped his phone. Two agents tackled him, slammed him face-first into the tile, and cuffed him tight.

An agent leaned close, shouting above the noise, "Carlos Ramirez—you are under arrest."

Carlos's eyes scanned the room in shock.

Jorge... was gone.

Just the echo of betrayal where his brother used to stand.

It's never the streets that get you.

It's the people.

The favors.

The ghosts.

Carlos wasn't caught counting bricks.

He was caught trusting the wrong ones.

CHAPTER 23

When The Feds Have You

That small room.

That cold room.

It makes everything flash before you.

Your mind can't stop racing.

Your gut tells you—*you messed up.*

And all you can do is wait.

Just wait.

When the feds have you, time stretches like scars.

Carlos sat alone in the narrow cell, head down, elbows on his knees, the echo of silence pressing in from all corners.

In his mind, he kept hearing *Leticia's voice*:

"I never liked Jorge..."

Then the sound of *Isabela's* joy from earlier that day:

"Daddy, you're coming to meet us for pizza, right?!"

Then his *young son's* small voice echoed in the back of his head:

"Can you kick the soccer ball after?"

Carlos closed his eyes, heart thudding like it was counting down something final.

The metal cell door creaked open.

A GUARD with dead eyes stood there, nodding. "On your feet. Let's go."

Carlos stood, wrists shackled, ankles chained. The hallway lights buzzed as he walked toward Room B7, where two agents sat waiting behind a gray metal desk. A blinking red light on the camera in the corner said everything Carlos needed to know.

CUT TO: PIZZA SPOT – WEST END ATLANTA

A small pizza parlor buzzed quietly. *Leticia*, *Isabela*, and *Aracely*—Carlos's sister—sat at a side table. The pizza grew cold in the center of the table. Nobody touched it.

Aracely leaned forward, brows pinched. "We need to ride by the townhouse. Something is not right."

Leticia checked her phone again. "He hasn't answered in two hours."

Aracely said, "I know he had a lot of money to count, but still. He could've picked up. Who was he meeting?"

Leticia looked up slowly. "Jorge."

Aracely blinked. "I know him. He is cool… they go way back."

Leticia leaned in, voice sharp. "I never liked him. Ever. Gave me bad vibes from day one."

Isabela pushed her chair back. "Let's ride. I feel it. Something's not right."

Leticia grabbed her purse. "Let's go."

CUT TO: INTERROGATION ROOM – FEDERAL COMPLEX

Carlos sat cuffed at the wrists, chains rattling lightly as he shifted. Two DEA agents, dressed in button-ups and cold purpose, leaned across the table. The air smelled like coffee, latex gloves, and stale justice.

Agent Tolliver, the taller Black agent with a southern twang, opened the dialogue:

"Look… give us your plug. You might get a break."

Carlos looked up, slowly.

"Nobody knows Heffy's movements. He is a ghost. He already got warrants on him for years. I only talk to his workers."

Agent Myers, pale, buzz-cut, flipped a folder open. "What about Jay and Slim? We are ready. We *want* them. How can you help us get them?"

Carlos tilted his head.

"That depends."

Tolliver leaned forward. "We already got some proffers on y'all. People talking. Deals being made. All we need from you is to bring 'em together. One room. Talk about the old days. Maybe throw out the idea of a new run. Let it sound like business as usual."

Carlos smirked faintly. "Let me talk to my lawyer first. I know how y'all move—*dirty backdoor deals*."

Myers tapped the table twice. "Clock's ticking, Carlos."

Carlos looked past them, eyes narrowing—not answering. Just calculating.

TOWNHOUSE – CASCADE AREA

Leticia, Aracely, and Isabela pulled up to the townhouse in Leticia's SUV. The driveway was empty. The front door cracked slightly.

They stepped inside.

Silence.
No Carlos.

No duffel bag.

Just open drawers, a few loose bills, and the faint hum of a money counter—still running.

Aracely held her chest. "He's gone…"

Isabela turned in circles. "He ain't pickin' up. None of this feels right."

Leticia pulled out her phone. "I'm calling the lawyer now."

They headed home as they pull up ten unmarked vehicles pulled up—all black Suv and cars

Agents jumped out flashing federal badges.

Agent Tolliver approached. "We got a warrant."

Leticia raised her hands. "I'm not resisting. I'll open the garage."

She tapped the remote.

The garage door creaked open.

Hours later Inside: money stacked in bundles. Duffle bags. Guns lined up in plain sight.

Tolliver turned to Myers, quietly. "This just bought us a promotion."

CELLBLOCK F – HOLDING WING

Carlos sat on the bottom bunk, staring at the concrete wall, his hand tapping lightly on his knee.

His *cellmate*, a quiet man with salt-and-pepper stubble named Reggie, looked over from the top bunk.

Carlos spoke first. "I need to use the phone. Why are they not letting me?"

Reggie grunted. "Cause they doin' something they don't want you stoppin' or warnin' nobody about."

Carlos stood up, went to the bars, shook them once. "I have a right to call my lawyer."

Reggie sat up, dangling his legs off the edge. "Yeah... in the streets maybe. This is the feds. They got 48 hours. They don't care about fairness."

Carlos paced the cell.

Reggie watched him.

"Are you new to this game?" he asked.

Carlos shook his head. "Nah. I just forgot how it feels to be hunted."

That room...

The cold one.

The one with the metal chairs and fluorescent lights.

That's the room where you finally understand—

The streets don't let you retire.

They just let you run... until you run out of time.

Chapter 24

Operation Three Kings

Friendship in the dope game?

To most hustlers, that word doesn't mean nothin'.
In a world of fake smiles and real charges, the linebacker numbers will make you go from *hard to soft* fast.
Landmines surround everything.
One wrong step?
You lose your life or your loyalty.

WEEKS LATER – ATLANTA

Carlos sat in a law office—gray carpet, wide window behind the desk, a faint hum from the central AC.

He was out on an ankle monitor, bonded out after putting up two homes and surrendering his passport.

Across from him sat his longtime defense attorney, Gerald Stanton, sleeves rolled up, eyes firm behind tortoise-shell glasses. A folder marked OPERATION: THREE KINGS sat in front of him.

Gerald leaned in.

"This is the deal," he said. "You throw your 50th birthday bash. Get all your old customers to come out. Get 'em talkin'. Let 'em engage in talk about past crimes… and future ones."

Carlos's face tightened. "So… set 'em up?"

Gerald nodded slowly. "You do that, and they'll give you 240 months."

Carlos squinted. "What? 240 months?"

Gerald tapped the folder. "Twenty years. Beats life."

Carlos looked away. "My son gon' be thirty. Daughter be damn near forty."

Gerald lowered his voice. "I tried to get more. Trust me. You only gettin' this break 'cause they got unfinished business with Jay and Slim. Y'all were under a sealed indictment. The whole thing's called *Operation Three Kings*."

Carlos exhaled through his nose, shaking his head slowly.

Gerald added, "But I'm not done fightin'. I got another call lined up with AUSA Henderson. If you play this right, you will still come home."

DOWNTOWN ATLANTA – PRIVATE RESTAURANT

Jay and Princess sat across from each other in a velvet booth, candles flickering low. Soft jazz played behind them.

Jay held his phone in one hand, showing Princess stock tickers. "The market dipped heavily. It's *buy time*, baby. Properties too. Gotta catch these steals."

Princess smiled. "I see you are still sharp with these numbers."

Jay's phone buzzed.

Carlos (on phone): "Yo, Low, what's good my brother!"

Jay grinned. "C-Lo! My guy. I'm good, man. What's the word?"

Carlos spoke smoothly. "Subdivision comin' along. Kids are good. Listen—I'm throwin' a lil' something for my 50th. Big yacht in Miami. Grown folks vibes. Need you there."

Jay leaned back, nodding. "Hell yeah. Been a minute. Say less—I'll be there."

From across the table, Princess gave him a playful side-eye. "Y'all better not be plottin' nothin' for *old time's sake.*"

Jay chuckled. "Nah, baby. Them days are dead. I love not lookin' over my shoulder."

SLIM'S HOUSE

Slim and Sierra lay tangled in the sheets, still breathless from a round of lovemaking. Moonlight spilled through the window.

Sierra climbed out of bed and walked to the bathroom, humming softly.

Slim's phone buzzed on the nightstand.

He grabbed it. "What's good?"

Carlos (on phone): "Slim, what up, fam. Wedding plans goin' smooth?"

Slim nodded. "Yeah, man. We gettin' everything locked in. My wash houses movin'. Just got two more contracts with new hotels."

Carlos replied, "Listen—I'm throwin' my 50th bash down in Miami. Yacht party. I need my day ones with me."

Slim smiled. "Say no more. I'm there. Can't wait to see you, bro. We gon' have a blast."

As he hung up, Sierra peeked around the bathroom door. "Who was that?"

Slim walked toward her, wrapping his arms around her waist. "C-Lo. He havin' a birthday bash in Miami."

Sierra leaned in, kissing him slowly. "Sounds like we got plans."

BACK AT CARLOS'S HOUSE

Carlos sat on the edge of the leather couch, his ankle monitor blinking softly. Across from him, Leticia sat in a robe, arms folded.

"So this what you have to do, baby?" she asked. "Set them up?"

Carlos nodded. "It's better for the family. I ain't proud of it. But they took over half a million from us. They got me by the balls, Leti."

Leticia exhaled, tears building in her eyes. "We gon' get through it. But I ain't gon' lie—this one hurt."

Carlos rubbed his hands together. "I know. And I'm still doin' time. Just not life."

Leticia walked over, kissed the top of his head. "Then you better make that party look real. But don't lose who you are in the process."

There's no loyalty in chess.

Only kings, pawns—and the pieces you're willing to sacrifice.

Carlos wasn't just throwing a birthday bash.

He was setting the table for betrayal.

And the feds?

They already lit the candles.

CHAPTER 25

THE PROFFER ROOM

Federal Building – Interview Room B3

The walls were blank. No clock. No window. Just pressure.

Carlos sat at a cold steel table, wrists cuffed in front of him. His lawyer, Gerald Stanton, sat beside him—calm, tight-lipped, his legal pad untouched. Across from them, two DEA agents adjusted a tripod-mounted camcorder. The red light blinked, waiting.

Agent Foster, older and composed, gave a slight nod toward Carlos.

"For the record, state your full name and date of birth."

Carlos cleared his throat. "Carlos Emmanuel Ramirez. Born July 8th, 1968. Age forty-nine."

Agent Davis leaned in, tone direct.

"Mr. Ramirez, you are now entering the proffer phase. You are required to disclose every crime you've committed—and who you committed it with. Leave nothing out."

Carlos looked at Gerald. No words were exchanged—just a long exhale.

Gerald gave him a subtle nod. "Go ahead."

Carlos shifted in his chair. The chains clinked softly as he straightened his back and stared directly into the blinking red eye of the recorder.

"Alright... from the beginning then."

He drew a deep breath.

"I started dealing in 1978. I was ten. It started with weed. My uncles, my mom, and my older brothers were all in—cutting, packing, loading trucks. Sometimes they let me take trips with them. I was making anywhere from two hundred to three hundred a week."

He paused, rubbed his palms on his jeans, and continued.

"By the time I was fourteen, they promoted me. I oversaw crops. Got a raise. More responsibility. But eventually, my uncles started moving heroin. They let me keep the weed side. I ran it."

Agent Foster raised an eyebrow. "Still in Mexico?"

Carlos nodded. "Back and forth. Mexico and Dallas. That's where I met my first wife. A war broke out between my uncles and the Sinaloa Cartel over territory and routes. Around '89. That ended with most of my uncles dead."

He swallowed.

"So I moved to Dallas full-time. I lived with my wife and her parents."

His voice lowered slightly.

"Between 1990 and 1994, I was moving two to five thousand pounds of weed a week when the season hit."

He reached for the cup of water in front of him, took a small sip, and leaned back.

"While in Dallas, cocaine started becoming the drug of choice. My customers were asking for it. My first delivery? Fifty kilos."

Agent Davis didn't flinch. "What did you pay?"

"Sixteen thousand a key."

"And what did you charge?"

"Twenty-two thousand."

Agent Foster stepped in. "So you were about twenty-two?"

"Yeah. My first child was on the way."

Carlos folded his hands slowly, the cuffs catching the light.

"Cocaine made more sense. Faster money. Easier to hide. Higher demand. Could never keep enough."

He blinked, staring at the floor for a beat.

"Things were good for a while. Me and my wife, we had two kids. Bought a ranch. Four cars. Money was flowing."

His tone shifted—hardened by memory.

"Until 1995. The Texas Rangers kicked in my doors. Took nearly everything. I got sentenced to 120 months. Did eight. Got deported."

Carlos's voice quieted. "Never saw my wife or kids again."

The agents exchanged a glance. Agent Foster pressed the pause button on the recorder.

"Let's stop there. One-hour break."

Carlos leaned forward, elbows on the table, eyes distant.

He wasn't a man speaking from regret.

He was a man speaking from survival.

FISHING TRIP-

Slim, Rico, and Bo sat on a pontoon boat with their sons. Fishing poles out. The breeze is soft. The sun is shining. The water is calm like the life they wished for their boys.

The dads weren't just teaching them how to cast a line—they were teaching survival.

SLIM: "Look around, son. This world wasn't built to love young Black boys. That's why I bring you out here. Peace doesn't always come to us—we gotta find it, make it, protect it."

Slim's son nodded slowly, eyes focused on his father.

BO: "And don't let that world convince you that being smart makes you soft. It makes you dangerous in the right way. Keep your eyes open, your name clean, and your circle small."

Rico leaned forward, talking to his son.

RICO: "College? Maybe. Maybe not. But learn a skill. Barbering, HVAC, welding, tech—something that nobody can take from you. Get a trade in your back pocket, and you'll never be broke again."

SLIM'S SON: "Dad, can I ask you something?"

SLIM: "Shoot."

SLIM'S SON: "What's the birds and bees?"

Slim laughed, shook his head.

SLIM: "You wanna know now? Alright. Listen close: it ain't just about sex. It's about responsibility. Your body, your choices, your future. Don't bring no life into this world until you are ready to love it, protect it, and feed it."

Rico added with a smile:

RICO: "Facts. Don't let lust detour you. Love your mind more than you chase what's between her legs."

The boys asked more questions. Real ones. About the police. About girls. About friends who turned fake. The fathers answered with truth.

BO: "You ain't just our sons. Y'all the seeds. You grow strong, we win. You get plucked too early—we all lose."

They sat in silence for a moment. Just the sound of water lapping the boat and fishing lines cutting air.

It wasn't just a fishing trip. It was a survival school.

SIDEWALK CAFÉ

The hum of morning traffic drifted past as Carlos and Gerald sat at a small wrought-iron table, two steaming cups of coffee between them. A light breeze stirred the edges of napkins and paper receipts on the sidewalk. The clatter of forks and distant laughter from other tables painted a scene that felt far too normal for the weight of their conversation.

Carlos leaned forward, his voice low but edged with worry.

"So I gotta tell them everything?"

Gerald didn't flinch. His suit jacket was draped neatly over the back of his chair, tie loosened just enough to show he'd been here before—too many times.

"Everything," Gerald said simply.

Carlos stared into his cup, swirling it like the answer might rise to the surface.

"What if I forget something?" he asked.

Gerald leaned in, voice firm but not unkind.

"If someone gets busted and brings up something you didn't mention... it can be used against you. That's how they play."

Carlos exhaled through his nose, eyes drifting to the street. People walked by, oblivious. Horns blared in the distance. Somewhere a siren wailed low, then vanished into city noise.

"Damn," Carlos muttered. "That's cold."

Gerald nodded once.

"It's federal. They don't care how it feels. Just what you say under oath."

Carlos nodded slowly, like the truth had finally landed. Not in theory, not in legalese—but in his chest.

For the first time, he understood:

Freedom wasn't a promise.

It was a process.

And someone else now held the keys.

CHAPTER 26

*The Backdoor Deals—The Ones You Never See Coming—
They're The Ones That Knock You Off Your Feet.*

FEDERAL BUILDING – INTERVIEW ROOM B3

Later That Day

The same sterile room. Same gray walls. Same camcorder blinking red in the corner. Carlos sat with his hands resting on the table. Gerald was to his left. Across from them sat the two DEA agents—Davis and Foster—each holding a notepad, the air around them thick with federal silence.

Agent Davis leaned forward.

"Pick up where you left off."

Carlos nodded slowly.

"I came home around 2004. Got sent back to Mexico after that sentence. That's when I bumped into Jorge."

"Jorge?" Agent Foster asked. "The same Jorge in this case?"

Carlos nodded again. "Yeah—the one who ended up setting me up."

He took another breath, a longer one this time.

"Jorge told me he had good things goin' on in Atlanta. Said he needed someone to run things. Said since I spoke English well, I'd be perfect."

Carlos's fingers drummed once on the table before stilling.

"He set me up. First thing he did? Sent 100 kilos. Plugged me in with some local buyers."

Agent Davis raised an eyebrow. "Mexican buyers or other?"

"Nah," Carlos replied. "All Black guys. Every one of them. They all had their own money. It wasn't long before we were moving 200, sometimes 300 kilos a week."

He shrugged.

"They were Jorge's people though… so I only saw a fraction of the money."

Carlos's jaw clenched for a second.

"Then Jorge showed up in Atlanta with his half-brother Felix. Told me flat-out he was takin' my spot. Said I needed to go get my own clients."

He looked up.

"One day, Felix asked me to ride with him to a dealership. While we are outside, a black-on-black 600 Benz pulls up. I didn't know him at the time, but out stepped Jay, his wife, and another woman."

Carlos's eyes narrowed, memory sharpening.

"I watched Jay real close. Said to myself, 'That's the one. He's my new lane.'"

"Where is Felix from?" Foster asked.

"Cali."

"Any dealings with him?"

Carlos shook his head. "Nah. Not beyond that."

He continued.

"Jay was there buying his and hers Range Rovers. One white. One black. Off the showroom floor. No games."

Carlos smiled faintly at the memory.

"So I made my move. I walked up to him, told him straight—I had 30 kilos in a hidden compartment in my car right now."

He leaned forward slightly, voice quieter now.

"Told him sixteen a key. Pure cocaine. Price he couldn't ignore."

Carlos lifted his eyes.

"Jay studied me for a second, then said, 'Let me see 'em. If they right, I'll buy them all right here.'"

"I pulled out two bricks. He checked 'em, broke a smile, and called his cousin—male—and told him to bring the money."

A beat passed.

"From there? We were locked in. Like hip to hip."

He paused, breathing out slowly.

"I finally started getting my own trucks after that. That's when I really started making money."

Agent Davis tapped his pen against his pad.

"How many keys was Jay buying by then?"

Carlos thought for a moment.

"Got to a point he was buying 125. Every ten days. Sometimes more. Sometimes I front him. It was clockwork…"

Agent Foster closed his notebook and glanced at the wall clock.

"Alright. Let's take fifteen."

The room emptied. The camcorder light faded to black.

DOCTOR'S OFFICE – MIDTOWN ATLANTA

Soft walls. Soft music. Soft lighting. But the tension in the room was sharp and tight.

Jay and Princess sat together in matching chairs. His hand covered hers. Her fingers trembled just slightly in his palm. The air smelled like disinfectant and flowers.

They'd been here before. Dozens of times. But today felt different.

A doctor stepped in, clipboard in hand, wearing a tailored smile.

"Princess..." she said warmly. "Congratulations. You're six weeks pregnant."

Princess gasped—one hand over her mouth, the other gripping Jay's. Her eyes filled with tears that couldn't decide whether to fall or float.

Jay froze, then stood up and wrapped her in his arms.

"This is the happiest I've ever been," she whispered into his shoulder.

"We did it, baby," Jay said, holding her tighter. "Finally."

Princess leaned back just enough to look up at him.

"When are you going to tell your other kids?"

Jay's face softened.

"Let's wait till you close to five, six months," he said. "Just to be sure."

She nodded, touching her belly lightly.

"I finally feel whole... as a woman."

Jay kissed her forehead.

"And we are about to be complete."

OUTSIDE INTERVIEW ROOM – FEDERAL BUILDING

Carlos stood just outside the closed door of Interview Room B3, phone pressed to his ear. The hallway buzzed with distant footsteps and the faint hum of overhead fluorescents.

On the other end, Leticia's voice came through, soft and steady.

"How's it going?" she asked.

Carlos took a breath. "It's going. Be done soon."

"I'm cooking," she said. "Your plate'll be hot when you get home."

A faint smile crept onto Carlos's face—tired, thin, but real.

Just then, the door cracked open. Agent Davis stepped out, nodding once.

"Let's finish."

Carlos ended the call without another word. He placed the phone in the tray by the door and walked back in, the weight of silence following him like a shadow.

Some deals don't need signatures.

The backdoor deals—the quiet ones, the unspoken ones—don't just shift the game.
 They erase the board.
 And by the time you realize what's gone...
 So are you.

CHAPTER 27

All you have in life is your word and the truth.

Back inside the room, Carlos picked up where he left off.

"So now, me and Jay rollin' in the dough. Jorge even tried to steal him from me. But Jay? He was like a golden goose—low-key, all about the hustle."

Carlos shifted in his seat, looking off as if seeing the past projected against the wall.

"One day, me and Jay and our families took a trip to Walt Disney World. While we were down there, we hit Clearwater Beach. While we were out on the beach with our families, that's when I first saw Slim. We didn't talk then—but later that night, at a restaurant, Slim and his family walked in."

Carlos smiled faintly. "Just so happened me and him were wearing the same watch. A Hublot. Knowing how much I spent on mine, I knew we had to connect."

He chuckled. "First we watched each other. Then we talked. I straight up asked him, 'How much you payin' a kilo?'"

One of the DEA agents held up a hand. "Where was Jay at this point? And what year are we in now?"

Carlos responded, "Jay stayed in his room—had too many drinks. This was around 2008. Obama had just become president."

Carlos continued, "Slim told me he was paying 23 a key. Buying 20 at a time. Delivery straight to his front door. Said he had St. Pete and part of Tampa on lock."

"I told him twenty per, still to his door. The rest was history. Took Slim maybe a year before he was buying a hundred every ten days. Before I knew it, I was moving 500 kilos regularly—300 to Jay, 200 to Slim. Like clockwork."

The agent asked, "Did the three of y'all take trips together?"

Carlos nodded. "Yeah, we took a few. Vegas, Cancun, even Dubai once. We moved smart."

"Were there guns involved?"

Carlos looked the agent in the eye. "Yeah, guns were around. Always are in this game. But no murders. Not to my knowledge."

Another agent leaned in. "Carlos, do you have any more properties, businesses, or cash we missed?"

Carlos hesitated, then shook his head. "No. What I told you is everything."

The agent studied him. "What about that truck that got pulled over in Augusta? Was that yours? Where was it going?"

Carlos sighed. "Yeah, that was mine. The load was headed first to Jay, then to Slim."

The agent scribbled on a notepad. "Can you pull them back in— or at least get them talkin' about the past?"

Carlos nodded slowly. "They both already agreed to come to my 50th birthday bash. I'm putting it together in Miami. They'll be there."

The agent clicked the recorder off. "Alright, Carlos. That's enough for today. We'll pick up later in the week."

AT HOME – LATER THAT NIGHT

Carlos sat at the kitchen table, his knee bouncing, eyes locked on a spot on the floor. Leticia, his wife, stood by the stove, stirring a pot of arroz con pollo.

She looked over, concerned. "What's wrong?"

Carlos looked up, voice low. "They asked about other businesses. If I had more money. I told them no… but that money's for y'all. Little over a million. All we have left."

Leticia walked over, stroked his hair softly.

"They'll be watching us," Carlos added. "My lawyer said we gotta move carefully."

Leticia nodded. "Then we do just that. Move quietly. The money's in a safe place. We just lay low till this over with."

They kissed. A silent bond between them forged in pressure, sealed in survival.

THE CALM BEFORE THE YACHT

Sometimes it's the quiet before the storm that tells you everything—the way people move, the decisions they make, the illusions they buy into. In the game of survival and legacy, every move is either a foundation… or a trap.

Jay and Princess were still in Atlanta, seated in a blacked-out Escalade parked outside a renovated brick duplex in Vine City. The air was thick with opportunity—and skepticism. They were meeting with *Renee Marshall*, a sharp, mid-30s Black real estate agent with silk press hair, a Cartier watch, and energy that let you know she didn't waste her time.

"This one right here just hit the market two days ago," Renee said, unlocking the security door. "The seller inherited it, and doesn't want to deal with the tenants. The asking price is $220K, but ARV—after repair value—is $365K if you do it right. Roof's less than five years old. Original hardwood under the laminate. This is a quick flip or a long-term rental, depending on how y'all want to play it."

Princess walked through the living room and peeped at the high ceilings and large front windows. "Feels bigger than I expected," she said.

Renee nodded. "That's 1,400 square feet, plus an unfinished basement you can turn into a separate unit. This neighborhood got historic protections, so the value only going up. I got investors making $3,500 a month renting to traveling nurses alone."

Jay looked around, took it in. "So if I put in, what, $25K in upgrades... I can flip this and walk away with a good $100K?"

"Easy," Renee said. "And I already got a contractor on standby who's worked with my people before."

Next stop was over in Pittsburgh—the Southside, where a fully renovated 3-bedroom sat on a quiet cul-de-sac. Asking price: $300K.

"This one already has tenants in place, paying $2,200 a month. They want to stay," Renee said. "And here's the kicker—it was appraised last year at $385K. So if you hold it for six months, refinance, you can pull out $60–70K tax-free and still have cash flow."

Princess looked impressed. "So we keep the renters, get the equity, and stay liquid?"

"Exactly," Renee smiled. "This is how y'all move into real estate freedom. Not just buying, but buying smart."

Jay said, "Alright, run us through the last one."

Renee drove them to the third spot, near the BeltLine in Adair Park—a two-bedroom bungalow listed for $175K. Small but clean, sitting on a corner lot with a new wooden fence.

"This one's all about location," she said. "You can turn it into an Airbnb easily. With the BeltLine three blocks away and Mercedes-

Benz Stadium ten minutes out, you're looking at $500 a night during events. Even on slow weekends, it stays booked."

Princess turned to Jay. "I say we take all three."

Jay nodded. "Cash deals. Let's make sure the title is clean and contractors lined up."

Renee shook both their hands. "Y'all won't regret this."

Just then, Jay's phone buzzed. He stepped aside.

"Low, what's good?"

It was *Yolanda*, mother of his two sons.

"Jermaine just got suspended. Again."

Jay rubbed his forehead. "Damn... I'll slide by later, talk to him. What about Jeremy?"

"He's cool. Straight A's like always."

Jay exhaled. "When you gon' let them stay with me, though? I'm still paying half child support."

"I'll think about it," Yolanda said, her voice clipped.

Back in the car, Jay relayed it to Princess.

"She said she might consider letting the boys move in. I told her I'd still pay half."

Princess looked out the window. "That's all she ever wanted— money. But this child is growing in me? I want Busy Bees."

They drove to Busy Bees, the old soul food spot that had survived gentrification and time. It was packed, just like it had been since Dr. King's era. Walls were covered with framed pictures of Black legends, and the aroma of fried chicken and baked mac and cheese filled the air.

Jay spotted *Westside Ken*, an old associate, sitting with a plate full of yams and oxtails.

"Man, the game ain't been the same since you left," Ken said, dapping Jay up. "But I know you got your reasons."

Jay grinned. "I made enough to fall back. Peace of mind is worth more now."

Ken chuckled, tapping his cane. "Yeah, well I hustle even when I'm limping. Ain't no retirement plan in the streets."

Both men laughed. Jay placed his order, then sat with Princess, soaking in the legacy of the moment—the money moves, the children, the life he fought to make clean.

In a world that glorifies speed and flash, the real win is longevity. Building something that lasts. Jay was learning that the right bricks lay not in fast flips or dirty dollars—but in foundations you don't have to lie about. And tomorrow... the yacht. But tonight, Atlanta still held him.

CHAPTER 28

RICH, POWER, AND DECEPTION

The glitter of money shines brightest before the fall. On the surface—luxury, laughter, loyalty. But beneath it? Riches, power, and deception.

The yacht floated off the Atlantic coast like a floating palace. Carlos had gone all out. Black Jack tables, a crab boil station, painted naked women serving top-shelf drinks, and the sweet bite of Cuban cigars drifting through the air. DEA agents posed as bartenders, waitresses, even crewmembers—all wired and ready.

Carlos worked the floor, wearing his charm like cologne. Laughing, patting backs, passing drinks. His energy screamed celebration, but his eyes scanned for reactions.

Jay and Slim stood near the rail, bourbon in hand, watching the skyline melt into twilight.

Jay: "Man, look at this. Who would've thought we'd make it this far, huh?"

Slim: (grinning) "Yeah. No more running. No more ducking. I actually sleep now."

They clinked glasses.

Jay: "You still remember Costa Rica? Them five girls we had—man, that little one, Amara? She used to cook with no clothes on."

Slim: (laughing) "And clean! And massage! That house was heaven. We were kings."

Jay: "Yeah, kings with too many enemies. I ain't mad we left."

Carlos walked up, grinning ear to ear.

Carlos: "Two of my favorite people in the world! C'mon now—y'all making me emotional."

Jay: "Happy 50th, brother. You laid this thing out."

Slim: "Yeah, you're moving like the money ain't run out."

Carlos: (chuckling) "And that's the problem—I'm spending like I still got bricks in motion. It's all going out, not enough coming back in. You know what they say..."

He leaned in.

Carlos: "We might need to make another run."

Jay narrowed his eyes.

Jay: "What?"

Carlos gestured for them to follow him. Inside a private lounge room, smoke swirled around the chandelier. A few guys lounged on velvet couches, cigars in mouths, lap dances in motion. A small speaker in the corner played salsa while someone in the back rapped quietly over the beat.

Carlos (raising his voice): "Man, I remember when y'all used to move a truckload before the sun came up. Hell, I got one loaded now. You could be back home before the feds blink."

One guy getting danced on chimed in:

Man: "Y'all should pick up where you left off. Ain't nobody moving like that no more."

Slim: "What them numbers looking like?"

Carlos: "Twenty-one a key. Going price? Twenty-six. Maybe more. Easy flip."

Slim: "Might talk to a few folks."

Jay: (shaking his head) "Y'all wild. I'm rusty. I got a baby on the way."

Carlos: "Y'all remember that drought in '09? We moved 500 keys in four days. Like magic. Money machine running all night. Naked women everywhere. Music blasting. That was life."

Slim: "Yeah... felt like gods."

They heard a shout from outside—

Guests: "Happy Birthday to you..."

Everyone joined in the singing. Carlos was pulled out to the deck for salsa dancing. Someone passed a tray of tequila shots, a few partygoers openly snorted lines of coke.

The DEA agents clicked photos, silently recorded.

Jay leaned in close to Slim.

Jay: "Something off with Carlos. He was glowing, but his spirit broke."

Slim: "Maybe he's hurting for real. Real estate probably is not going as planned. He is trying to get us back in the game."

Jay: "You thinking about it?"

Slim: "Fifty-fifty. If it lines up right... maybe."

The crab game opened near the back deck. Slim rolled first, cracking jokes. Jay bet a few racks, laughing. Carlos slapped bills on the table, pretending he didn't just offer betrayal in champagne.

The night was beautiful. The water is calm. Music is rich. But the truth? The boat was wired, and the game was bait. And loyalty, like a pair of dice, was rolling loose.

CHAPTER 29

Reflection is a strange thing—it shows you what you missed, what you ignored, and what you never thought would circle back. Inside those gray walls, where time moves slowly and thoughts grow loud, you start seeing the truth with sharper eyes.

The present day, Atlanta Federal Detention Center—the air thick with tension, the floors waxed but stained by stories.

Jay leaned against the wall in the day room, eyes watching the muted television hanging overhead. Slim, now known inside as Drake, sat beside him.

"Man," Jay said low, "my gut tellin' me Low set us up."

Drake cocked an eyebrow. "Why do you say that?"

Jay rubbed the side of his face, as if trying to wipe away the memory. "Just reflecting. That night... all that loud talk 'bout the past and future. Low never talks like that around people. Never."

Drake shrugged. "I charged it to him bein' drunk. Had the Henny in his system."

Jay shook his head. "Nah, bro. The vibe was off. The man barely made eye contact. All he wanted to talk about was the 'good old days'... and what we 'could' do next. Then boom. Two years later—we sittin' in this box."

OG Lamont, a tall, seasoned inmate in his sixties with skin like sandpaper and wisdom heavy in his walk, strolled over.

"Let me holla at y'all for a second," Lamont said, pulling up a plastic chair. His voice was calm, but sharp enough to cut steel.

"Be careful who you talk around in here. Folks ear hustle and try to jump on your case just to get time shaved off theirs. Trust me,

I saw it. They'll take the stand, sing like birds, and you won't know until you hear your own name on the paperwork."

Jay nodded slowly. "I heard somethin' like that before."

Lamont leaned in. "Look, I ain't sayin' y'all gotta plead guilty. But just know—the longer your case stays open, the more vulnerable you become. Superseding indictments. Add-on charges. Folks you ain't even think mattered start poppin' up. It's chess, not checkers."

Drake rubbed his chin. "We waitin' on discovery right now."

"Your lawyer should have that soon. But truth be told?" Lamont said, looking from one to the other, "You don't really need a lawyer unless you takin' it to trial. This Fed game doesn't play like state court. There ain't no room for magic tricks. You get what the guidelines say—unless you got somethin' to trade."

Jay leaned forward. "My lawyer said the conspiracy charge is tied with relevant conduct which enhancements my biggest fight."

"That's 'cause y'all been hit with ghost dope," Lamont replied, almost whispering now.

"Ghost dope?" Drake echoed.

Lamont looked them both square in the eyes. "Yeah. That's when folks you never got caught with still swear under oath what you moved—just enough to bury you. Prosecutors take that to the grand jury. You never in the room, never hear it. But it's your name they callin'."

Jay sat back. "Damn. That's cold."

Lamont stood. "Cold? That ain't the half. This system ain't built on fair—it's built on deals. Deals made in rooms you never step foot in. Keep your head down. Watch who talkin'. And remember—this ain't about truth, it's about narrative. They already writin' the story. Your job now... is to not let 'em write the ending."

Jay and Drake sat in silence, the weight of Lamont's words settling heavy over them like a winter coat.

Later that evening Princess was in the bed, her mother bringing her a glass of juice.

Princess said, "I don't want to raise my child alone."

Delores said gently, "Right now just focus on having a healthy baby."

Princess said, "Mom, Jay was doing everything right. Completely changed man. Why would God allow this to happen? He was so involved with sponsoring the underprivileged kids."

Delores said, "We can't question God. Just have to be strong. Jay is a good man. I'm sure God won't give him more than he can bear."

Princess sighed, placing a hand on her stomach. "This is just unfair. We waited so long for me to become pregnant."

Carlos was at home enjoying himself with his son in the backyard, kicking the soccer ball. His son, ten years old, was laughing, chasing the ball across the lawn. The grill was sizzling with carne asada, and upbeat Mexican music played from a Bluetooth speaker.

On the porch, Leticia sat with their daughter watching the two.

Leticia said, "We have to be there for Rodriguez when Carlos leaves."

Isabella said, "Mom... we ladies. How? I don't play soccer."

Leticia smiled and said, "We have to be there emotionally for him. Make him feel supported. That's what matters."

They both watched silently as Carlos lifted his son into the air, spinning him around in a circle as the boy laughed, the sound cutting through the weight that hovered over them.

Carlos and his son kicked the ball across the grass, laughing as it rolled too far and the boy chased it toward the bushes. The smell of grilled carne asada danced through the air, the radio playing Vicente Fernández in the background. Leticia and their daughter sat on the porch steps sipping Jarritos, watching the moment like it was sacred.

Suddenly, the sound of tires on gravel broke the rhythm.

Two black marshal cars rolled up the driveway. Doors opened.

The music stopped. The boy stopped. Leticia stood.

Carlos stepped forward, confused, wiping his hands on his jeans. One of the marshals flashed a paper.

THE AGREEMENT

They came early—too early.

Carlos stepped out onto the porch in sandals and a T-shirt, a half-drunk cup of coffee in his hand. The sun hadn't even fully broken the sky when the two federal marshals approached the gate.

The taller one spoke first, voice even and firm.

"Mr. Ramirez. We're here to take you in."

Carlos blinked, then stiffened.

"What? I still got ninety days left—I got a deal. Check with my lawyer!"

The second marshal didn't break stride. "The order's been updated. We're just here to follow it."

Carlos backed up slightly, tension rising in his voice.

"This ain't right! You can't just show up unannounced—I got a family, you hear me? Let me call my lawyer!"

From behind the screen door, Leticia pushed her way out, still tying her robe.

"This is wrong!" she shouted. "He did everything y'all asked! You said we had ninety more days!"

Isabella joined her, panic in her eyes. "You can't take him like this!"

The marshals didn't flinch. The taller one opened the back door of the black government SUV with the kind of indifference that said they'd done this a hundred times.

Carlos's son stood frozen by the curb, clutching his soccer ball like it was the only thing holding his world together. His eyes stayed fixed as the marshals placed his father in the back seat.

Carlos twisted in the cuffs, shouting over his shoulder.

"Call the lawyer! Tell him they're breaking the agreement! This is a mistake! You hear me—this is a mistake!"

The door slammed. The vehicle pulled off.

No one moved. For a long, hollow moment, silence filled the space where Carlos had stood just seconds earlier.

Leticia slowly wrapped her arms around their son's shoulders. He didn't speak. His grip loosened.

The soccer ball fell from his hands and rolled quietly into the street.

In the belly of the system, truth becomes a rumor, loyalty becomes currency, and silence becomes survival. And even the strongest men learn—the real time starts long before the sentence drops. It starts when your name gets whispered behind a door you didn't open.

CHAPTER 30

WHEN BEING REAL COSTS YOU

Jay sat across from his lawyer, Trent Maxwell, in the small consultation room. The table between them was crowded with manila folders, scribbled notes, and over a thousand pages of discovery.

Jay ran his fingers through his hair and exhaled. "Man... this discovery is thick. Over a thousand pages. I'm gonna need more time to go through it all, but what I've read so far—it's mostly hearsay. Ain't no real proof, just people talking."

Maxwell nodded grimly. "That's the sad part. In federal court, hearsay counts. They allow conspiracy to breathe off people's words alone."

Jay shook his head. "Crazy part—all these blacked-out names, look like the heat came from Carlos's side. That car pulled over May of 2012 on hwy 75 south had Derrick who got pulled over. It looks like he gave statements. This whole thing is dirty."

Maxwell flipped a few pages. "From what I can tell, over twenty people gave proffers on all three of y'all. This case was dead until Carlos' yacht party—that's what gave them the knock-out punch. Your plug got caught up in another case, and when he cooperated, they reopened the 'Three Kings' file. Y'all had the feds beat... until then."

Jay's eyes darkened. "I'm taking this to trial. I wanna look every snitch in the face. I want 'em to say my name while I stare back."

Maxwell hesitated. "That's a big risk, Jay. With this many people talkin', and your name across that much paper? You're lookin' at 30 to life if found guilty."

Jay leaned back. "What's the plea?"

"Twenty years. First offense, they shaved some time off. But if you lose in court…"

Jay looked him square in the eye. "Get prepared. We goin' to trial."

In the rec yard, Drake leaned against the fence, talking with OG Lamont, a battle-worn inmate who'd been through more trials than most defense lawyers.

"Lamont, this whole system is fake, man," Drake said. "My plug told on us on some old shit. There's no drugs. No money. Just hearsay. And they still got us."

Lamont nodded like he'd seen it all before. "That's federal court. Have you ever heard of *ghost dope*?"

Drake frowned. "Ghost what?"

"Ghost dope. They take what people *say* you sold and build a number from that. Then they bring in witnesses and say, 'how much do you think he moved?' They use that to stack your time."

Lamont pulled out a pen and used a scrap of napkin to do some math.
 "You said you moved 50 bricks a week for four years? Look— 50 bricks a week, 52 weeks a year. That's 2,600 a year. Times 4? That's 10,400 bricks."

Drake grabbed his stomach. "Damn…"

Lamont nodded. "That's how they bury you. And then they hit you with enhancements—leadership role, firearm proximity, money laundering. Have you ever made threats?"

"Nah," Drake shook his head quickly.

"Good. 'Cause threats or violence would get you another bump. But look—accepting responsibility knocks off two points. Having a GED or diploma? More points off. It's a game of numbers. You want the lowest guideline possible before the judge picks a number."

Meanwhile, at another FDC, Carlos sat in a legal booth with his attorney, Samuel Rojas.

Carlos looked tired. His hands trembled slightly.

"I'm gonna have to take the stand, ain't I?" Carlos said quietly.

"Only if they take it to trial," Rojas replied. "But yeah, it's lookin' like you'll have to."

Carlos looked down. "Damn… this messed up. We were boys. Me, Jay, Slim… I never thought it would come to this."

Samuel leaned forward. "Carlos, you're still facing 240 months. That's twenty years. The feds don't care about loyalty. They care about leverage. You got one shot to tell your side before they paint you however they want."

Carlos swallowed. "I got a wife. A ten-year-old son. I just want to make it back home."

"Then focus. If you go down, make sure it ain't for something you didn't do."

Carlos nodded slowly, the weight of his choices thick in his chest.

Inside the downtown field office, the two lead DEA agents sat across from each other in a glass conference room littered with case files, photos, wiretap printouts, and timelines drawn in red ink across the whiteboard. A pot of stale coffee steamed between them as they reviewed the latest update from the U.S. Attorney's office.

Agent Barnes, flipping through Jay's discovery folder, spoke first. "You think we can get Jay or Drake to flip? If either one gives us a list of who they supplied… that's our RICO case."

Agent Velez leaned back, arms folded, a crooked smile tugging at his face.

"Pressure's on now. Nobody wants to do time. Once the fear sinks in, they start thinking differently. Hell, some of 'em tell on their own momma and daddy."

Barnes chuckled. "Facts. I've seen guys turn on their childhood best friend over a five-year sentence. It's wild—when the feds walk in, street loyalty walks out."

Velez lit a cigarette and took a drag, glancing over the timeline pinned to the wall.

"Carlos gave us the layout. We got twenty-plus witnesses. Now we just need to get 'em all sayin' the same thing."

Barnes leaned forward, tapping a manila folder labeled Operation: Three Kings.

"You think they actually takin' it to trial?"

Velez shook his head slowly.

"Doubt it. They'd be fools. We got too many people pointin' fingers. Nobody survives that. It's not a matter of if—they just gotta pick who goes down first."

Barnes looked toward the mirror glass, where surveillance footage of the yacht party played on loop. Jay laughed. Slim tipping the dealer. Carlos grinning wide with a cigar in his hand.

Velez exhaled smoke, eyes still fixed on the screen.

"We just gotta make sure the witnesses are all on the same page when it's time."

This is how the system breaks you—not with truth, but with pressure. They don't need the facts. Just fear. A name. A rumor. A nod in the dark. In this game, being real doesn't save you… it buries you.

Chapter 31

THE COST OF TRUTH

Sometimes the loudest evidence ain't what's said in court—it's what they already decided in silence. And when the truth gets expensive, only the ones built for the fire dare to speak it.

Jay and Drake sat shoulder to shoulder in the echo-filled day room. Metal chairs scraping the tile, dominoes slapping on nearby tables, the sound of reality bouncing off concrete walls.

Jay leaned forward, elbows on his knees, voice low. "Think I'm taking this to trial."

Drake looked up from his commissary sheet, brow furrowed. "Man... that could mean life. And life in the feds? That means exactly that. No do-overs. No parole."

Jay nodded slowly, almost as if he'd already made peace with the idea.
"I know. But look at the paperwork, bro. If it wasn't for that damn yacht party, they really don't got us. It's our word against everybody that's flippin'. Ain't no product. Ain't no money. Just noise."

Drake exhaled hard and rubbed his face with both hands.

"I ain't gon' lie. I'm pleadin' out. Before all these other cats try jumpin' on our case, stackin' lies to get a deal."

Jay gave a tight nod, not judging—just listening.

"I feel you. Each man gotta move how he moves. But me? I want to look every last one of them in the face. I need that."

Drake hesitated, then spoke slower.

"Jay… truth is? We were out there. Hustlin'. No, they ain't catch us red-handed. But we were out there. And they got folks talkin'. Pointin'. You know how this system moves. Don't take much to bury a Black man in the feds."

Jay looked away for a moment, eyes fixed on the fence outside the window.

"I know. But I've been buryin' parts of myself for years. Not this time."

Across the room, chaos broke the air. Two inmates high off K2—better known as deuce—were lost in another reality. One of them crawled across the concrete like he was swimming, arms making breaststroke motions as if he were deep in the Atlantic. The other stood, nodding out, eyes rolling back until he lost control of his body—urinating on himself in front of everyone.

Some inmates burst into laughter. Others just shook their heads, used to the madness.

Jay shook his head, disgusted.

"Man… this our next twenty years? Shit crazy. Nothin' but a lotta junkies in the feds now."

Drake sighed.

"That 2K took over. Real ones get buried under paperwork. And this the circus left behind."

Jay turned to him.

"How are you? Are you able to leave them straight?"

Drake nodded.

"Yeah, but you know how it is when the head ain't around. Hopin' Sierra can manage everything, hold it down."

Jay looked off again, his mind drifting.

"I had just invested a lil' over a million into real estate. I'm done pumpin' money into the music game. They gon' have to make it work. Got some stocks and bonds tucked too."

Drake nodded.

"I got a few properties and them wash houses runnin'. Still... shit don't hit the same from in here."

A crowd of inmates had surrounded the deuce heads now. Someone had pulled out a contraband cell phone and was recording it—going live like it was entertainment.

east side Decatur, Sierra sat at the dinner table with her sister. Her fork sat untouched.

"I'ma have to get back to Tampa soon," Sierra said, voice heavy. "The boys need me. My friend Tasha watchin' them for me."

Her sister, Monique, reached across the table.

 "Sis... just take it one day at a time."

Sierra wiped the corner of her eye.

"That's all I can do. But twenty years? That shit hurt me to the core. Every time I think about it... it breaks my heart."

Westside Atlanta, Coach Love stood talking with a few other coaches outside the rec center.

"Don't look good for Jay," Love said, arms folded. "He left enough money to keep the kids' program runnin' for the rest of the year, but after that? It's gon' get rough."

Coach Dee shook his head.

"Crazy how they come for him years later. The man was a changed man. Sponsored tournaments, kids, scholarships..."

"The Feds don't care about any of that," Love muttered. "Once you are in their crosshairs—it's game time."

They say doin' right will erase your wrongs. But in the Fed's playbook, redemption doesn't mean nothin' when your past got weight. And now, Jay and Drake had to decide—hold the line, or bend before the system snaps them in half.

CHAPTER 32

The price of being real is often paid in silence, isolation, and the weight of loyalty. In the federal system, you either stand tall on your word or drown in the games the government plays. There are no half-truths when the walls close in—just decisions that echo for decades.

Drake sat across from his lawyer and two DEA agents in a small concrete room. The lawyer broke the silence.

"I came with some good news," he said, unfolding a stack of documents. "They're willing to lessen your charges if you give them some evidence. That way, you could be looking at 120 months, if you give them something solid."

Drake looked over at the agents.

One of the agents tossed a manila folder across the table. It opened to reveal a few surveillance stills. "Recognize any of these fellas?"

Drake stared calmly. "I never kicked it with them before."

"You sure?" the agent asked, raising an eyebrow. He pulled another photo from the file—a shot of Drake in a club talking with one of the men.

"I didn't say I didn't know them. I said I never kicked it with them."

"You mean to deal with them?"

"However you want to word it," Drake said, his jaw tightening.

The agent leaned in. "What do the streets say about them? Heard they took over Tampa after you stepped down."

Drake shook his head. "I'm here to accept my responsibility for what y'all got on me. That's it."

His lawyer placed a hand on his arm. "Drake, this could really help you—"

Drake cut him off. "Then why the hell am I paying you to tell me to snitch? You want to dirty my name?"

The agent laughed. "I've seen your kind. When y'all get down the road, sitting with thirty years, you wish you did snitch. But it will be too late."

Drake stood up. "Are we done here or what?"

Back in the dorm, OG Lamont was in the middle of his federal law breakdown. Jay sat at the chess table, half-listening while playing his game.

"Y'all better understand the system," Lamont said, voice carrying. "That 851 enhancement? That's when you got a prior drug conviction. They file that—you getting hit twice as hard."

"What about that 924(c)?" a young inmate asked.

"Guns with drugs," Lamont said. "That's a mandatory five years stacked on top of your sentence. You got more than one gun? They'll run that back-to-back. Nine-two-four-G? That's gun possession for career criminals. Don't get caught with nothing if you got priors."

Another inmate leaned in. "Ghost dope, OG?"

Lamont shook his head. "That's when people say what you moved, even if they never caught you with it. They get three witnesses saying you moved a hundred keys? That's what you are getting sentenced on. No dope. No pictures. No text. Just their words."

Jay moved a rook, still absorbing. "That's how they do it. A court without you ever being in it."

Lamont nodded. "Grand jury. All they need is enough whispers to turn them into a case. And every snitch is just trying to save their own skin."

The dorm went quiet for a second.

Jay sat in his cell later that night, finally getting a call in to Princess.

"How are you holding up, bae?" he asked.

Her voice cracked. "I'm just holding in a lot of anger. Why you, Jay? With all these bad people out here..."

"I know, right? But I need you to be strong. It's two of y'all now. He or she can't defend themself yet. They depend on you."

"I know... I'll do better," she sniffled. "I haven't even been eating lately. Your boys called. Said they want to come over."

"That'd be good. I'll call them later. Look, our story doesn't end here—we are just passing through this storm."

"I didn't plan on raising our child alone, Jay... if they have their way, our unborn baby will be grown before you come home."

Jay went silent. The words hit like a freight train.

"I think about that every day," he finally whispered. "But just know I'm fighting them every step of the way."

Drake came stomping back into the dorm, face tight.

Jay, who'd just gotten off the phone, looked up. "You good?"

"Hell naw. I want to fire my damn lawyer. Just called me up there trying to get me to snitch on P-Rock, Rico... even point the finger at you. Why in the hell did I give him a hundred stacks?"

Jay sighed. "The games they play, bro. I fired my first one for the same reason. Told him to kiss my ass."

In federal prison, freedom is rarely measured by days or months. It's counted in dignity, choices, and how well you can sleep at night knowing you didn't fold. For men like Jay and Drake, the hardest part isn't the time—it's watching the system turn your name into a weapon against your own people.

CHAPTER 33

VOWS IN THE SHADOWS

There's a moment in every hustler's life when memory feels sharper than the steel around his wrists. When loyalty becomes more than a word—it becomes the only currency left. For Jay, that moment came with the weight of regret, the sound of federal doors closing, and a vision from the past he couldn't shake.

Jay leaned back on the cold bench in the dayroom, his eyes half-closed, drifting into a vivid flashback. The air smelled of bleach and old sweat, but in his mind, he was back at that car lot—sun shining, grills flashing.

FLASHBACK — ATLANTA — CAR LOT — DAY

Carlos walked Jay through the back, past rows of foreign whips. He nodded toward the Range Rovers.

"That one for her. That black one, for me ," Jay grinned.

Jay watched Carlos pop the trunk on his whip.

"I got 30 bricks, clean. Pure."

Jay didn't flinch. He pulled out his phone and called his cousin.

"Bring the bag. All of it. 480K."

45 minutes later, a matte-gray truck pulled up. His cousin stepped out with two duffels. Carlos opened one, sliced into the corner of a brick with a pocketknife. Jay nodded.

"Done."

From that moment on, ATL wasn't just a playground. It was theirs.

INT. MIDTOWN CONDO — NIGHT

Carlos and Jay were counting millions. Cash laid like bricks of war across the marble counter.

Carlos looked up, serious.

"I need 600K. Jorge acting funny. Say he not fronting me any more."

Jay didn't blink. He slid a Louis Vuitton duffel across the table.

"We brothers. You already know."

Carlos sat back, nodding.

"You are more realer than blood."

They toasted.

EXT. MIAMI — JET SKIS & BALCONY — NIGHT

Jay, Carlos, and Drake flew through the waves, then kicked back that night on a Miami balcony. Blunts burning. Champagne pouring. Their women inside were laughing.

Carlos raised a glass.

"If one of us falls... the others take care of his family."

Jay raised his.

"I am my brother's keeper."

Drake raised his own.

"To death do us part. We married by the game."

Moments later, Carlos sat with his head low.

"I just took a 1.5 loss."

Jay looked at Drake.

"I got 300 for you."

Drake nodded. "I got 250."

They tapped glasses again.

INT. CONDO — NIGHT

Jay slammed a folder shut.

"That's the third truck pulled in 60 days. The one in Augusta almost sank us. Maybe it's time."

Carlos sighed. "Might be right."

"We made enough. Let's go legit. Raise our kids. Watch our money grow. Can't spend nothing behind bars."

Carlos nodded slowly. "I'll talk to Drake. After this... we're out."

PRESENT DAY — SIX MONTHS LATER — FEDERAL TRANSPORT VAN

A GUARD slammed the bars on the van's interior.

"Clean y'all mess up!"

Jay stirred, his head still leaning against the cold steel wall. He looked up. Outside the small window, the courthouse rose like a mountain he didn't want to climb.

They pulled up. One by one, the inmates were led out, shackled and silent.

INT. COURTHOUSE HOLDING CELL — MORNING

Jay stood in the cramped holding cell with five others. One inmate paced like a madman, sweat soaking through his orange jumpsuit.

"Man, the jury found me guilty. Facing 260 months. They were bullshit. I ain't even blink wrong. They made up their minds before I said a word."

The tension clung like smoke.

A guard opened the cell door.

"Jason Collins. Let's go."

Jay looked at the floor, then up at the sky through the narrow slit of light in the wall. His body moved, but his mind remained on that balcony, glass in hand, loyalty in heart.

THE TRIAL BEGINS

United States District Court – Northern District of Georgia – Atlanta Division

Case No. 1:24-CR-298

United States of America v. Jason Demarcus Collins

Jay stood in the holding tank, staring at the floor. His suit was pressed tight. A federal officer unlocked the steel door and called out:

"Jason Collins. Let's go. Trial's starting."

He stepped into the corridor, wrists shackled, escorted to the adjacent holding prep room. His defense attorney, Trent Maxwell, was already there, flipping through the trial binder.

"Morning, Jason," Trent said. "The jury's seated. I like the balance. Seven women, five men. Mostly Black and Hispanic. You keep your head up in there. Federal trials ain't about who you are—they about what they say you did. You got this?"

Jay nodded slowly.

"Just keep calm," Trent continued. "No reactions. No talking across the room. Look at me or the jury, not the witnesses. Especially not him."

He tapped the first name on the witness list.

"Derrick Matthews."

Jay's jaw clenched.

They entered Courtroom 1907, on the 19th floor of the Richard B. Russell Federal Building. The courtroom was packed. Princess sat front row beside Jay's mother and sons. His sister and two brothers were behind them. The public gallery was nearly full.

"All rise," the clerk announced.

The Honorable Judge Michael T. Randle entered from chambers.

"The United States District Court for the Northern District of Georgia is now in session," the clerk declared. "The Honorable Judge Michael T. Randle presiding."

"Please be seated," said Judge Randle. "Let's proceed. Clerk, read the case."

"Case number 1:24-cr-298, United States of America versus Jason Demarcus Collins," the clerk read aloud. "Charges under Title 21, United States Code, Sections 841(a)(1), 846, and 851—Conspiracy to Distribute Controlled Substances."

"Government, call your first witness."

AUSA Kimberly Phelps stood. She wore a sharp navy suit and held a yellow legal pad.

"The government calls Derrick Matthews to the stand, Your Honor."

The side door opened. Derrick walked in slowly. He wore a brown DOC jumpsuit—an inmate in custody, hair freshly braided, chains clinking at his waist and ankles.

Jay looked straight at him. No smile. No nod. Just silence.

"Do you swear to tell the truth, the whole truth, and nothing but the truth, so help you God?" the clerk asked.

"I do," Derrick replied.

"Please state your name, age, and current status for the record," Phelps said.

"Derrick Matthews. I'm thirty-eight. Currently incarcerated at USP Coleman, Florida."

"Do you know the defendant, Mr. Jason Collins?"

"Yes, ma'am."

"How long have you known him?"

"Over ten years. We met in Atlanta around 2010. I was hustling, he was hustling."

"Have you ever purchased narcotics from Mr. Collins?"

"Yes. Multiple times."

"Can you be specific?"

"From 2011 to 2017—on and off. Moving kilos of Cocaine."

"In May 2012, were you arrested on I-20 with ten kilos of cocaine?"

"Yes, ma'am."

"Who did you obtain that cocaine from?"

"Jason Collins."

"Is Mr. Collins present in this courtroom today?"

"Yes." Derrick pointed. "That's him right there."

Jay looked dead at him, jaw locked tight.

"No further questions at this time," said AUSA Phelps.

"Defense may cross," Judge Randle said.

Trent stood, straightening his jacket. He stepped slowly toward the witness stand.

"Mr. Matthews, you're facing federal time, correct?"

"Yes."

"What were you facing before you decided to cooperate?"

"Twenty-five to life."

"And what were you promised in exchange for testifying today?"

"Freedom."

"Freedom?" Trent repeated.

"Yes, sir."

"Let me be clear—you're testifying today not because you were caught, not because of guilt, but because the government gave you a deal?"

"I agreed to cooperate to save myself."

"How many times have you been convicted of felonies?"

"Three."

"You'd say you're pretty familiar with what gets you time off?"

"Yes."

"No further questions, Your Honor."

Trent returned to his seat. Jay looked over at his mother—she hadn't moved. Eyes locked forward, silent prayer in her stare.

The past doesn't die. It lingers—rotting in the bones of those who thought they could outrun it. And loyalty? Loyalty costs more than money. Sometimes, it costs the only thing a man truly owns: his freedom.

CHAPTER 34

"THE WEIGHT OF TRUTH"

There are choices that bend a man's spirit, and others that break it. In the dorms of Atlanta FDC, no one wore guilt or pride plainly. Everything was quiet calculation. And in federal courtrooms, truth was no longer about fact—it was about who could make a jury believe.

Lies on the Stand
United States District Court – Northern District of Georgia
Case No. 1:24-CR-298 – United States of America v. Jason Demarcus Collins

ATLANTA FDC – DAYROOM – SAME DAY

Drake sat across from OG Lamont on a plastic stool. Above them, the television flickered with muted CNN reruns. A low hum filled the air—some inmates paced, others played chess, a few nodded off in corners.

"I went ahead and pleaded guilty, man," Drake said. "I ain't got the balls like Jay."

OG Lamont nodded, folding his arms across his chest. "You did the right thing. The feds ain't in the business of letting you beat 'em. They don't take losses well."

Drake ran a hand over his head. "So what do you think I'm looking at?"

"Twelve to fourteen," Lamont said. "It just depends on your case manager. Truth be told, they hold the key to your halfway house, your camp placement, and damn near your out-date."

Drake stared off, quiet for a long moment. "I just hope my boy comes out right. Jay is a good dude. All this... it just doesn't feel real."

INT. U.S. DISTRICT COURTROOM – LATER THAT WEEK

The courtroom was packed. U.S. Marshals stood posted along the walls. Jason sat at the defense table beside his attorney, Trent Maxwell. His suit was dark navy, crisp. His cuffs had been removed, but tension pulled tight at his shoulders.

"All rise," the clerk called.

The Honorable Judge Michael T. Randle entered in black robes, face unreadable.

"Court is now in session," the judge announced. "The United States versus Jason Demarcus Collins, case number 1:24-cr-298. Prosecution, call your next witness."

AUSA Kimberly Phelps stood, holding a crisp yellow pad.

"The government calls Jimmy White."

A tall, stocky man entered wearing a faded DOC jumpsuit, tattoos creeping above his collar. He raised his right hand as the clerk administered the oath.

"Do you swear to tell the truth, the whole truth, and nothing but the truth, so help you God?"

"Yes, ma'am."

He took the stand.

"Mr. White," Phelps began, "please tell the court why you're here today."

"I was arrested in Augusta transporting five hundred kilos of cocaine," Jimmy said. "I was driving a commercial truck."

"Who gave you the narcotics?"

"They loaded it at a warehouse in Bakersfield, California. Been using that warehouse a while."

"Where were you delivering the shipment?"

"Warehouse off Fulton Industrial Boulevard here in Atlanta."

"And who were you delivering the shipment to?"

"The instructions said to ask for 'Black.' But I knew it was for a guy named Jason."

Jay didn't flinch. His eyes stayed locked straight ahead.

"How many times did you make this delivery?"

"Over two years."

"Thank you. No further questions."

Phelps sat down. Maxwell rose from the defense table, walking with purpose.

"Mr. White, I want to remind you—you're under oath. Lying in this courtroom is a federal crime. Understand?"

"Yes, sir."

"In those two years of delivering shipments, did you ever meet my client—Jason Collins?"

"No, sir."

"Did you ever receive a single payment, text message, phone call, or instruction directly from Mr. Collins?"

"No."

"So your claim is that you believe you were delivering to him— despite never seeing him, never speaking to him, and never being paid by him?"

"That's correct."

"How much were you being paid per delivery?"

"A hundred thousand a load."

"And how much time were you facing when you were arrested?"

"Life."

"And the government offered you what—reduction in sentence if you gave them names?"

"Yes, sir."

"Thank you. No further questions."

Maxwell returned to his seat. Phelps didn't blink. She simply adjusted her notes.

"The government calls Leonard 'Len' Barrow, currently incarcerated at USP McCreary, Kentucky."

A thin man entered, walking with a slight limp. He was sworn in, took the stand.

"Mr. Barrow," Phelps said, "where did you first meet Jason Collins?"

"Magic City. Back in April 2013. We were in VIP. He was with some folks—real flashy."

"And what happened there?"

"We partied. After a few drinks, I asked him what he charged for a brick. He said thirty-four flat. I started buying from him after that."

Jay raised an eyebrow, leaned slightly toward Maxwell.

"Never seen this man in my life," he whispered.

Maxwell stood. Calm. Precise.

"Mr. Barrow, let me be clear—you claim to have met Mr. Collins at Magic City, April 2013?"

"That's correct."

Maxwell pulled a document from his file folder.

"This is Mr. Collins' U.S. passport. Shows he was in Africa and Europe for the entire month of April 2013. Hotel records, flight itineraries, stamps. So tell the jury—how did you meet a man in Atlanta who was 4,000 miles away?"

Len froze.

"And while we're at it," Maxwell continued, "this is your incarceration record. You were booked in the Fulton County Jail from March 12 to May 7, 2013. Care to explain that?"

"I... I might've got the dates mixed up..." Len stammered.

"You mixed up jail with Magic City?" Maxwell paused. "Not likely."

Judge Randle peered over his glasses. The jury whispered among themselves.

Maxwell held both exhibits high, then calmly returned to his seat.

Some truths carry weight. Others unravel the moment you put them on the stand. That day in court, Jay didn't just look confident—he looked clean. And in the eyes of the jury, sometimes all it takes is one lie under oath to burn the whole building down.

CHAPTER 35

THE TRIAL WITHIN THE WALLS

The walls of Atlanta FDC held more than inmates. They held reflections, regrets, and revelations. For Jay, the courtroom wasn't the only place a trial was unfolding. There was one happening every time he opened his mouth, every time his name was whispered through the federal airwaves. But on this particular day, he felt something rare inside those steel-bolted walls—relief.

Jay sat on the plastic bench in the dayroom across from Drake and OG Lamont. A soft murmur of dominoes slapping and TVs humming surrounded them. He leaned forward, eyes steady.

"Can't even lie, I'm feeling good about how this trial is going," Jay said. "Some dude I didn't even know took the stand. We ate him alive—lunch meat. Caught all kinds of lies. Hell, he picked a year and month when I was out of the country for the whole thirty days."

Drake leaned back, folding his arms. "Good, glad to hear that. Shit, I signed off on my plea. Ain't no turning back now."

OG Lamont nodded slowly. "Make sure your lawyer keeps his foot on their neck. That's the key."

Jay nodded. "I got three of them. Ain't no letting up."

Just then, a tall, stocky man in his mid-50s with cocoa-brown skin and a salt-and-pepper beard approached. His prison greens were creased like a doctor's coat. Everyone called him Doc. Drake spotted him first.

"Doc, tell OG them how they did you."

Doc let out a frustrated breath. "Man, they sent fake patients into my clinic trying to get me to prescribe to them. I saw through it. Shut it down. Then they doubled back, claiming I was overmedicating folks who were in car wrecks, had job injuries. Straight set up."

OG Lamont shook his head. "That's the feds' new hustle. I ain't never seen this many doctors come through the system."

"It's a chess move," Doc said. "They hit doctors under 21 U.S.C. §841, treating us like street dealers. Just 'cause we ain't slinging bags on corners doesn't mean they won't twist it like we are."

OG nodded. "I remember the Dr. Shakeel Kahn case. Feds hit him with conspiracy, distribution, and even a continuing criminal enterprise charge. Man got life."

Doc grunted. "Exactly. And now they tryin' it with me. Offered me 120 months. I told them to crank it up. I'm taking it to trial."

Jay leaned in. "What's their play, Doc?"

"Control," he said. "Plain and simple. See, when we stop writing them scripts, the same folks in pain gon' hit the streets. And when they hit the streets? They overdose. Then the same government that put us in here—they act surprised."

OG Lamont added, "It's bigger than pills. It's about power. Keep the doctors scared, they back off. Keep the sick desperate, they reach out. And every overdose? Another reason for more funding, more policy, more control."

Jay stared off. "Damn. I always thought this system was crooked, but this is the next level."

"This ain't about guilt," Doc said. "It's about leverage. They want a story. A conviction. Headlines. Not the truth."

Drake sighed. "What's scary is, even with the truth, we still might lose."

The three men fell silent for a moment. Just the buzz of fluorescent lights above, and a guard yelling count time in the distance.

Outside, the world kept spinning. Inside, time stood still.

Scene: Upscale Lounge in Downtown Atlanta – 9:23 PM
PHELPS sat in a dimly lit booth with two of her colleagues, Assistant U.S. Attorney Monica Raye and Investigator Thomas Weller. A jazz quartet played softly in the background as wine glasses clinked and case files sat quietly in their briefcases under the table.

Monica leaned forward. "So, where are you on United States v. Jason Collins? Thought that was gonna be a slam dunk."

PHELPS took a slow sip of her red wine and exhaled. "I'll be honest—one of the key witnesses fell apart on the stand. Full of holes. Lied about a date when Collins wasn't even in the country. Judge Maxwell looked like he smelled bad shrimp."

Thomas raised an eyebrow. "Didn't your office vet the guy?"

"I should've cross-checked his timeline more thoroughly," PHELPS admitted. "He heard about Jason through hearsay or some bunk jailhouse pipeline. I should've known better. This one's slipping."

Monica smirked. "Happens to the best of us. But if you need leverage..."

Thomas cut in, "What about superseding the indictment? Throw something at his wife. She tied in, right?"

PHELPS looked up, intrigued. "Princess? She had access to the accounts, luxury cars in her name, and wore diamonds this case paid for."

Thomas nodded. "Pull her bank statements, Venmo history, shell LLCs. You know the play. That might make Jason fold fast. He won't let his child be born while his wife is sitting in the feds."

Monica tilted her glass. "Apply pressure. Make him sweat. This case could land you the Eastern Division lead next spring."

PHELPS sat back, gears turning. "Yeah... Jason Collins might have fought his whole life, but we are about to fight back federal-style."

Grady Memorial Hospital – Labor &

Delivery Wing – 10:45 PM

Princess clutched her belly as the wheelchair raced through the sliding double doors. Her water had broken in the car. Nurses moved fast.

Her mother Delores held her hand, whispering, "Just breathe baby girl. In through the nose... out through the mouth. You are strong. You a Collins."

Jay's mother Miss Rosa stood across the hallway, praying aloud, "Lord, surround my grandbaby with angels. Let her come through safely and whole."

Princess screamed through another contraction. Her sister Danielle wiped sweat from her forehead. "C'mon sis. You are almost there. You got this. Jay's with you in spirit."

Nurse Chambers checked vitals. "She's dilated to nine centimeters. Baby's on the way!"

Monitors beeped. The tension was electric. Princess gritted her teeth, tears mixing with sweat. "He should be here," she whispered.

Danielle kissed her cheek. "He is. In every heartbeat."

SCENE: FDC ATLANTA – CELL BLOCK C – 11:08 PM

Jay sat on the edge of his bunk, flipping through a Bible when his Tracfone buzzed quietly. A message popped up from Miss Rosa:

"She's in labor. They just wheeled her in. Pray."

Jay stood, heart racing. He turned to Drake who was lying on the top bunk, staring at the ceiling.

"My wife's about to have our baby."

Drake sat up, eyes wide. "Man, that's what's up. Congratulations. I know how hard y'all been praying on that."

Jay nodded slowly. "Yeah… just wish I could hold her hand."

He texted back: "I'm here. I love y'all. Tell her to breathe for both of us."

Drake leaned back. "Do you ever think about how America has one of the highest incarceration rates in the world… yet we are only 5% of the global population?"

Jay exhaled, "They never broke the chains, just swapped 'em for contracts. All they know is the cage."

Drake nodded. "Yeah. The whole system is designed for us to fail before we start."

Jay looked out the slit window, stars barely visible. "But not this time. My daughter gon' be born into love—not just struggle."

Some wars are fought in courtrooms. Others, in the mind. But when both collide behind bars, you find out what you're really made of. And sometimes, what you refuse to be broken by, becomes your only salvation.

CHAPTER 36

A PACT BROKEN

Carlos Ramirez leaned against the steel bunk, his voice low and heavy as he spoke to Hector Morales, another inmate-turned-informant. Both men had walked away from everything they once built—money, power, family—trading loyalty for leniency. The overhead light buzzed softly, casting shadows across the concrete walls of the Mexican-run pod.

"I really hate I flipped on Jay and Drake," Carlos muttered, his accent thick with regret. "Jay... man, he's the reason I got rich. Met him, and I shot straight to the top. Never crossed me, always solid. A real brother."

Hector nodded but didn't look at him. Instead, he watched the movement in the dayroom through the thin vertical slot of their cell door.

"As long as you didn't tell on another Mexican," Hector said quietly, "you good with us. In our book, you didn't snitch."

Carlos sighed. "I know... I know. But I keep thinking about that night in Miami. On the balcony. We made a pact. We swore if one of us fell, the others would take care of the family."

Outside the cell, loud Spanish chatter echoed through the tier. A group of ten Mexicans gathered by the microwave area, laughing, making homemade pizzas out of commissary ramen, chips, and squeeze cheese. Over in the Black section, a few men were playing chess and Spades. The TV area was mostly white boys—some watching reruns, others clearly spun out on meth or nodding from K2, still upright but barely living.

Carlos and Hector stepped out of their cell and into the chaos. The smells of burnt noodles, old socks, and sweat clung to the air. Carlos grabbed a slice of the pizza, nodding at a younger homie who offered it up.

Carlos spoke through a mouthful of food, his words muffled but clear enough.

"I hit the stand next week," he said, wiping sauce from his chin. "Gotta put on a show. They want me to bury Jay."

Héctor, seated across from him with a styrofoam cup of instant coffee, chuckled.

"Frío, cabrón. Luego regresas con tu familia."

(Fry his ass. Then get back home to your family.)

Another Mexican—older, with faded tattoos and a dark Santa Muerte inked along the side of his neck—chimed in from behind them.
"Ojalá tuviera a alguien para delatar. Solo regreso al viento."

(I wish I had one to snitch on. I'll be going back to nothing but the wind.)

They laughed, throaty and careless, scraping their trays with the kind of boldness only rats and deals could buy. But just a few feet away, at the chess table near the far end of the chow hall, the Black inmates weren't laughing.

"You hear that shit?" Marlo asked, leaning toward his homie TJ. His frame was tall, wiry, with a twisted dread bun hanging low off the back of his head.

"Hell yeah, I heard," TJ replied, eyes narrowing like the thought alone left a bad taste. "They bragging about snitching on us... in Spanish. Like we stupid."

Marlo clicked his tongue. "Man, they really think we dumb."

He leaned back slowly, nodding once, the gears turning. "Time to show 'em we speak more than one language."

They stood up quietly. TJ wrapped a National Geographic magazine around his stomach with torn sheets and tucked a dictionary across his chest. Another Black inmate, K-Low, did the same. They didn't talk. They strapped up.

Back near the microwaves, the Mexican pod boss—El Lobo—was cracking jokes when Marlo walked up, standing face to face with him.

"I heard everything," Marlo said, calm but cutting. "Y'all braggin' about droppin' dimes on us. Laughin' like we're some damn fools."

Lobo stared back. For a moment, the dorm held its breath. Then Lobo smirked, nodded slightly, and said something fast in Spanish to his crew.

That's when it happened.

TJ stepped from the side and cracked one of the young Mexicans in the face. The boy dropped like a sack of rice. Lobo tried to counter, but Marlo ducked, lifted, and slammed him into the metal bench. Knives flashed—long, sharpened toothbrushes from the Mexicans, jailhouse ice picks from the Black crew.

The fight was explosive.

Carlos got caught in the middle. He tried to crawl under a table but took a steel tray to the ribs before someone booted him in the face. Blood dripped from his nose as he curled up, arms over his head.

"On the ground! On the ground!"

The COs stormed in. Mace sprayed in all directions. Everyone hit the floor or caught a boot to the back. Two inmates were leaking blood from their arms, another unconscious near the TV.

It took seven guards, two riot shields, and a full lockdown to get control.

Back in his cell, Carlos sat on the toilet, an ice pack pressed to his eye.

"I knew this was coming," he whispered. "But not like this. Not from them."

Hector, now pacing in his boxers, shook his head. "Told you. Blood loyalty means something here. You broke the code, bro. Now you gotta survive it."

Loyalty is easy to shout when the sun is shining and the millions are flowing. But in the belly of the beast, behind steel bars and layered lies, loyalty is a debt paid in bruises, betrayal, and blood. Carlos broke the pact—and the streets never forget when you do. The war inside the walls had begun. And this time, it was personal.

CHAPTER 37

THE SOUND OF NEW LIFE

The silence in the hospital room was thick with emotion. Princess lay in her bed, one arm wrapped gently around her swaddled newborn daughter, eyes filled with tears that blurred the boundaries between joy and sadness. She had given birth to a healthy, beautiful girl—but Jay wasn't there to see it. He wasn't there to cut the cord, to hold her hand, or whisper words of love and comfort into her ear.

Her mother, Delores, stood at her bedside beaming with grandmotherly pride. She gently stroked the baby's soft cheek and smiled. "She's got your glow, Princess. But those eyes—those belong to Jay."

Jay's mother, Rosa, sat on the other side of the bed, rocking gently. "Her nose is definitely yours, but that fire in her face? That's my son. That's Jay all day."

They all laughed softly, and for a moment the pain was replaced by peace. Princess whispered, "Her name is Jamie Beyoncé Collins."

Delores nodded. "Strong name for a strong little queen."

Rose added, "She gon' make noise in this world, just like her daddy."

Princess's phone vibrated. She quickly answered.

"Jay?" she whispered.

His voice crackled through the line, filled with emotion. "She looks just like me, huh?"

Princess chuckled through tears. "Yeah. But with my mouth and nose. Jay, she's perfect."

Jay exhaled, the sound heavy. "Damn. I just wish I could hold her. Smell her. Kiss both of you."

"She got your eyes, Jay. Real strong. She stared at me like she knew the whole world already."

Jay closed his eyes, imagining it all. "What you name her?"

"Jamie Beyoncé Collins."

Jay smiled on the other end. "You went full royalty."

"Their grandmas already got her whole next 18 years planned," Princess said, laughing.

"That sounds just like them," Jay said, his tone warm despite the pain. "What about the deals?"

Princess leaned back. "Went through clean. Rehab on track. Two houses closed last Friday."

Jay felt pride swell in his chest. "That's what I'm talking about. Even from here... we are still building."

The sun was hot and loud at the park. Cleats scraped across red clay. The youth baseball league had just clinched a spot one game away from the World Series. Energy buzzed like a live wire.

Coach Love stood in front of the boys, wiping sweat from his forehead. His voice cracked with emotion as he spoke. "This one... this win... it's for Coach Jay."

The boys raised their fists. "Coach Jay!" they yelled in unison.

Assistant coaches stepped up, offering words of encouragement. Coach Dee added, "Jay ain't just put money up—he put his heart in y'all. Remember that when you are on that field."

The team captain, a tall, lean 13-year-old named Tre, stepped forward. "Coach Jay believed in us when nobody did. Let's win the whole thing for him."

"Coach Jay!" they roared again.

Later, as the crowd dispersed, Coach Love leaned against his truck, watching the boys load gear into vans. Coach Mitchell approached him with a folder in hand.

"Yo, Love," he said. "Been thinking about something. You know that empty space on Cascade near the old barbershop?"

"Yeah," Love replied, squinting. "Why?"

"Thinking about opening a bar. Classy joint. Chill vibes. But I can't do it alone. You in?"

Coach Love rubbed his chin. "Bring the blueprint. Let's talk. I'm open. We need something to keep us building, too."

Across town, Big Cheese stood in the studio with DG, Bossman, and a few others. The walls vibrated with bass. Tracks poured out of the speakers like gasoline on fire.

"Radio spins going up," Big Cheese said. "Social media numbers are climbing. Now it's time to take over the streets. We goin' harder."

DG leaned forward. "My IG and Snap lit right now. Real fans tapping in. Not just bots."

Bossman nodded. "I've been in these clubs. DJs spinning us without asking. Folks requesting us by name."

Big Cheese looked around the room. "We are doing this for Coach Jay. He put us in position. It's time to pay him back."

DG nodded with conviction. "Coach believed in me when I was lost. He didn't judge. He gave me purpose."

Bossman added, "He risked it all for us. Let's risk it all to return that favor."

Big Cheese raised his hand like a general. "Goal is Birthday Bash. Hot 107.9. That stage is ours next year."

DG said, "Bet. Let's kick the door down."

From the delivery room to the dugout, from the studio to street corners of Atlanta, Jay's fingerprints were still all over the lives he'd touched. Though his body was locked away, his spirit moved through every goal scored, every track dropped, every brick laid in the rebuild. And in that quiet breath between hope and heartbreak, his name still rang loud.

Coach. Brother. Father. Visionary. Jay Collins was still in the game. Just playing from the shadows now.

CHAPTER 38

BROKEN CODES AND BACKDOORS

In Tampa, Florida, the sun was heavy and unforgiving. The heat clung to skin like desperation. Inside a faded brick house on the east side, two old friends sat plotting—caught between survival and betrayal.

Rico leaned over the table, sweat beading on his neck. "I talked to Slim," he said, voice low. "He took the plea. 240 months."

Bud raised an eyebrow. "Wait... how many years is that?"

Rico tapped his phone. "That's twenty. He might do fifteen with a good time."

Bud shook his head slowly. "Damn. He got himself in some real shit."

"Better him than us," Rico said, his tone dry but heavy.

Bud rubbed his hands together. "Still... twenty years. That's a whole damn life."

Rico nodded. "And now the money is dry. We need to bust a move—fast."

Bud looked at him. "What are you thinking?"

"I got a lick lined up. Easy money. Sweet too."

Bud leaned in. "Yeah? Spit it."

Rico met his eyes. "Sierra. Slim left her sitting on at least 250K. Maybe more."

Bud blinked. "Slim fiancée Sierra?"

"Yup," Rico said. "He made all that money, smashed all the baddest chicks, then just stopped pushing when Jay and Carlos told him to chill. Left us high and dry."

"Like they his handlers," Bud muttered. "He really jumped when they said jump."

"I'm sliding through tomorrow," Rico said. "She just got back to town. I'ma throw the ball with the boys, act normal... feel the house out."

Bud smirked. "Play uncle. Get inside. I like it."

Rico stood. "We make this clean, we up again."

Sierra stood in her quiet house, the weight of the past year pressing on her chest. Her wedding dress still hung untouched in the hallway, like a ghost of a future that never arrived. The house was clean but quiet—too quiet.

She whispered to herself, pacing. "I didn't plan for this... not this part."

The front door swung open and broke her thoughts.

"Mom!" shouted Lil D and TJ as they rushed inside, backpacks bouncing.

She dropped to her knees, hugging both tightly. "Hey, my babies."

"Daddy didn't come back with you?" TJ asked, his eyes big, his voice hopeful.

Sierra's throat tightened. "No, sweetheart. Daddy's going to be gone for a little while. But we'll get to visit him. Okay?"

"Was Daddy a bad guy?" TJ asked, softly.

Sierra held his face. "No, baby. Your daddy just got caught up around the wrong people. He's still a good man."

Lil D, now 12, stepped forward, his voice stronger than before. "I just want to see him. I miss him."

Tasha walked in behind them, carrying groceries. "I see y'all beat me inside."

Sierra smiled tiredly. "They've been missing him badly."

Tasha sat on the armrest. "You good?"

"I'm holding it," Sierra said. "Barely I'm trying to figure it all out. Being mom and dad, the bills, the business

They sat in silence for a moment. Then Sierra's phone buzzed.

Rico: Hey sis, just checking on you and the boys. Y'all good?

Sierra: Yep. Just made it home. We are all here chillin.

Rico: Cool. I might stop by tomorrow. Throw the ball with the boys. Bring my lil man.

Sierra: That'd be great.

She turned to Tasha. "I always liked Rico. Real dude. Only one who's actually checked on us since Drake got locked."

Tasha didn't hide her skepticism. "Yeah, Rico cool. But I don't trust anybody these days. People change when money dries up."

"You right," Sierra said, heading toward the kitchen. "Let's drink to fake friends and real ones."

She poured two glasses of Henny, turned on some Brandy, and handed Tasha her cup. "To better days."

Tasha raised her glass. "And even better nights."

They sipped, laughed, and let the music carry them—for the moment, the world outside could wait.

Sometimes the danger doesn't knock—it texts first. Loyalty, grief, and survival were never meant to walk in the same room. But in the south... sometimes they have to. Especially when vultures fly low and old friends stop by with smiles too wide.

CHAPTER 39

Some courtroom battles are fought with facts. Others fought with fire. And then, there are those rare battles where the facts are the fire—burning through lies, exposing deals, and turning entire cases to ash.

Jay's legal team sat around a long mahogany conference table, papers spread like war maps. Attorney Maxwell tapped a file with his pen. "We have a real shot at a mistrial. Len took the stand under oath and lied—blatantly."

Attorney Foster nodded, flipping open his laptop. "We pulled surveillance, passport records, travel stamps, and verified hotel logs. Jay wasn't even in the country the entire month Len claimed he met him."

"We need to push the motion based on perjury," Maxwell added. "There's precedence—U.S. v. Cervantes, 200 F.3d 1101 (7th Cir. 2000)—key witness lied, the conviction got reversed."

Another attorney chimed in, pulling up cases. "Also Napue v. Illinois, 360 U.S. 264. If the government knowingly uses false testimony, or fails to correct it, it violates due process."

"It's our opening," Maxwell said. "Len was their key witness, and nobody else has been able to place Jason at the scene, in the business, or in the conspiracy. He's a ghost in their own case."

They all nodded. A motion for mistrial was being drafted before the coffee went cold.

Outside, at a suburban Atlanta park, Jay's two sons passed a basketball back and forth on the blacktop.

"You think Dad's gonna be home by our graduation?" Jeremy asked, his voice quiet but full of hope.

Jermaine paused, bouncing the ball with a frown. "I hope so. He said he was gonna buy me that Charger for my birthday."

Jeremy kicked at a loose rock. "I wish Mom would let us stay with him before... it's gonna be different without him here now."

Jermaine nodded. "Yeah... we got a new sister too."

"I know," Jeremy said. "Grandma Rosa told me."

They stood silent for a beat, brothers on the verge of becoming men, carrying questions too heavy for their age.

Inside Atlanta FDC, the vibe was different. Institutional lights buzzed overhead, casting a pale blue across the concrete floor. Jay and Drake were posted near a table with a chessboard, while Bone and Bullet joined them in casual conversation.

"Man, I remember when you pulled up to Club Vision in that V12 AMG Benz on 24s," Bone said, laughing. "Shut the whole place down."

Jay grinned, shaking his head. "That was All-Star Weekend. But I didn't shut it down—BMF did. AG made so much money, he said he had to stay 'til Monday 'til the bank opened. Had 'em send a Brink's truck."

Bullet whistled. "That's when the A was the real A. Hustlers getting money, shining for real."

Jay chuckled. "Man, we hit Magic City first. My first time seeing BMF that deep. Champagne showers."

Drake chimed in. "I drove up from Tampa that weekend. ATL was off the chain."

Bone leaned in, lowering his voice. "You had a good run, Jay. Hate that we connected in here, but your name rings bells, trust me."

Jay's face grew more serious. "That's not always a good thing in here. Your past is your worst enemy. If I could do it all over... I'd have laid low. Played it smart. The Feds don't play fair."

Bullet said, "I can't lie. After I knock out this bid, I'm gonna try again."

Drake looked up, shaking his head. "You a better man than me. I'm done. I'm about to miss my son's graduation. Might even miss my grandbaby's first steps."

Jay exhaled deeply. "Yeah. Me and these folks been throwing punches since day one. It's draining. Some days I feel like I'm swinging with no arms."

The silence between them held the weight of time, regrets, and choices made under a sky that once seemed full of stars.

Sometimes, the past comes dressed like a victory. Other times, it sneaks in with a knife. For Jay, the court wasn't just a fight for freedom—it was a reckoning with every deal, every move, and every person that ever whispered loyalty... or betrayal.

And as the motion for mistrial took shape, so did something else: the smallest sliver of hope.

But hope, like freedom, always came with a price.

CHAPTER 40

LINES IN THE SAND

Rico pulled up to Drake's house just after noon, the Florida heat bouncing off the windshield as he shut the car door. The hum of cicadas filled the air. Sierra answered the door wearing sweats, her hair tied up in a loose bun. She looked tired, but her eyes lit up when she saw Rico.

"Where is your son at?" she asked.

"Had to go somewhere with his mom," Rico replied, stepping inside. " He wanted come"

She nodded and stepped aside. "Thanks, Rico. For real. Not many have been checking on us."

The boys came bounding down the stairs—TJ and Lil D, both with footballs under their arms like they'd been waiting for this moment.

"Let's hit the yard," Rico said, slapping palms with both of them.

Sierra smiled. "I have some business to handle on the phone, but I'll be out in a minute."

Outside, Rico lined the boys up and started working them through drills. "You gotta cut sharp, like this," he said, demonstrating a route. "Uncle Rico gon' always be here for y'all, feel me? If you ever need me—anything—you hit my line."

The boys nodded, locked in.

Sierra eventually stepped outside, phone in hand. "It's for you," she said, handing it over.

Rico put the phone to his ear. "What's good, my dawg?"

Drake's voice came through with warmth. "Boy, I miss your ass. Real talk."

"Man, same here. Been keepin' an eye on the fam for you."

Drake replied, "That means a lot. I'm puttin' a real play together for us, you're going to run the operation ."

"You already know I'm in. We been down since high school. Just playin' my part. How they treatin' you in there?"

Drake exhaled. "It's solid. I'm cool. Kickin' it with some real ones. Sierra said she thinkin' 'bout movin' close to wherever I get shipped. Unless they send me to Coleman Low."

Rico chuckled. "Damn, she movin' away from me?"

"Yeah," Drake said, laughing. "But I need you to run the business while I'm down. I'll give you 20% of the profits. Plus, I wanna buy a few dump trucks. We'll chop that up, too."

Rico nodded. "Say less. Just keep me posted."

Meanwhile, Coach Teddy Love was out front, washing his car, reggae music humming low from a Bluetooth speaker. The water hose snaked along the driveway, soap suds sliding off the hood of his Dodge Charger.

An unmarked black SUV rolled up slowly. Love noticed immediately, narrowing his eyes as two DEA agents stepped out.

One flashed his badge. "Teddy Love? We're with the Drug Enforcement Administration."

Love didn't flinch. "What can I do for y'all?"

Agent Miller stepped forward. "We're gonna need you in court next week."

Love turned off the hose, drying his hands on a rag. "Court? For what?"

Agent Miller pulled a file from his briefcase. "You remember the statement you wrote about Jason Collins? From back when we caught you with five keys?"

Love sighed. "That was nine years ago. You can't be serious."

Agent Miller remained firm. "We're dead serious. You named him as your supplier in a signed affidavit. Now we need you to take the stand."

"Not a chance," Love said, voice rising. "I'm not testifying to anybody. That was paperwork to save my ass back then. That doesn't mean it was the truth."

The second agent, Agent Daniels, chimed in. "We've got financial records—paper trails from Jason to you. Large deposits. Two cars in your name. That box truck business you both had shares in. If you don't cooperate, we can supersede. Hit you with new charges—money laundering, conspiracy. You'd be looking at federal time, not state."

Love shook his head in disbelief. "Man... this some lame-ass shit. I can't believe y'all."

Agent Miller stepped in close. "Make the right decision. We'll be in touch."

They walked back to the SUV, leaving Love standing in his driveway, towel in hand, cursing under his breath.

Back inside the FDC, Jay and Drake were laughing in the dayroom, reminiscing.

"Man, remember Cancun?" Drake said, shaking his head.

Jay grinned. "How could I forget? Rico fell off that jet ski, I lost a twenty-thousand-dollar bracelet in the ocean, and Dice got arrested in Mexico."

"Ten racks to get him out," Drake added. "Still can't believe that."

"Carlos kept talkin' 'bout he was ready to get back to the States," Jay said, laughing harder now. "He said, 'Too much excitement, papi. I need Atlanta traffic again.'"

Drake leaned back. "Best and worst trip of our lives."

Jay nodded. "No doubt. But man, moments like that? Worth more than the monCan't believe Carlos put us on the cross"

Sometimes memories are the only currency a man can spend when his freedom's been robbed. And sometimes, those memories remind him of what's still worth fighting for.

CHAPTER 41

THE MOTION TO STRIKE

In the hushed chambers of Federal Judge Michael T. Harrison, the air was heavy with tension. Leather-bound law books lined the paneled walls, and the ticking of a brass desk clock felt like a countdown to something irreversible.

Maxwell leaned forward across the polished oak table, eyes sharp behind wire-frame glasses. "Your Honor, I'm filing for mistrial under Rule 33 of the Federal Rules of Criminal Procedure. Our motion rests on newly discovered evidence that proves one of the prosecution's primary witnesses—Leonard Griffin—committed perjury on the stand."

Judge Harrison nodded slowly. "Go on."

Maxwell's voice never wavered. "Mr. Griffin testified he met my client, Jason Collins, in April 2013 at Magic City in Atlanta. Our defense presented travel records, passport entries, and hotel confirmations proving Mr. Collins was out of the country—Africa and then Europe—for that entire month. The government's own flight data corroborates this. That witness lied under oath, and his testimony served as a cornerstone for the prosecution's case."

Across the room, Assistant U.S. Attorney Carla Phelps sat cool, but her foot tapped quietly under the table.

"That's a stretch, Counselor," she finally said. "Even if Griffin's timeline was off, we have six more witnesses set to testify—each of them independently tying Mr. Collins to this drug trafficking operation. A motion for mistrial is premature, inflammatory, and an overreaction to a single witness misremembering a date."

188 | GHOST DOPE

"Mis-remembering a date?" Maxwell leaned back, incredulous. "He didn't forget the color of a car, Ms. Phelps—he placed my client at the center of a conspiracy, in a city he probably wasn't in. That's not a minor discrepancy. That's fabricated testimony. False statements from a key government witness violate my client's Sixth Amendment rights and obstruct the integrity of this trial."

Judge Harrison raised a hand to still them. "Ms. Phelps, the Defense has produced documentation verified by federal systems, including CBP reentry records. Do you dispute the accuracy of those travel logs?"

Phelps crossed her legs, flipping through a manila folder. "We're not contesting the travel logs. But a trial is not a microscope for perfect memory—it's a cumulative review of evidence. Mr. Griffin's testimony was not our entire case. The defense cherry-picks one inconsistency and wants the whole thing thrown out."

"Your Honor," Maxwell said, voice rising slightly, "the issue isn't whether Griffin was forgetful—the issue is that the government put him on the stand knowing his account couldn't be corroborated. That amounts to willful negligence at best, and at worst, prosecutorial misconduct. And if the next six witnesses are cut from the same cloth, this trial becomes theater, not justice."

Phelps cut in. "We're not staging anything, Your Honor. We're prepared to call cooperating co-conspirators, DEA task force agents, and warehouse documentation clerks who handled shipping manifests tied directly to Mr. Collins's properties in both Fulton County and Stockton, California. There's a pattern here. The Defense cherry-picks one inconsistency and wants the whole thing thrown out."

Judge Harrison exhaled, eyes shifting from one side to the other. "This court takes perjury seriously—especially when it impacts a defendant's right to a fair trial. But a mistrial is a nuclear remedy. At this time, I am not granting the motion."

Maxwell opened his mouth to respond, but the judge raised a hand.

"However… The court will strike Mr. Griffin's testimony from the record and instruct the jury to disregard it entirely. If it emerges that additional witnesses knowingly give false or misleading statements, this court reserves the right to revisit the matter. You'll reconvene in court one hour from now."

He stood, robes flowing.

"Ms. Phelps, I advise you to vet your remaining witnesses thoroughly. Mr. Maxwell, be ready. The court adjourned—for now."

As the attorneys gathered their papers, Phelps locked eyes with Maxwell for just a moment.

"Six more, counselor," she whispered.

Maxwell responded just as quietly. "Six lies don't make one truth."

The courtroom was packed when the session resumed. Jason's entire family filled the gallery—his mother Rosa, his father, his sister. Only his wife, Princess, was missing, still recovering in the hospital after giving birth to their daughter.

Phelps stood. "The government calls Damon Richards to the stand."

A man with a confident walk and clean-cut clothes took the oath and sat. Jason stared at him, stunned. A deep silence fell over his thoughts as a memory came flooding back...

Jason stood on a wooden porch, handing an envelope of cash to a soft-spoken older woman.

"Miss Richards, this is for Dice. And something extra for you too," Jason said, voice respectful.

"Baby, you a good friend," she replied, clutching the envelope. "Don't find too many like you. Ever since he's been locked up, you've been lookin' out for him."

"Me and Dice are like brothers," Jason said. "I told him— whatever he was going through—I got his back."

Back in the courtroom, Jason clenched his jaw. Dice wrote statements on me? His heart dropped like an anchor in dark water.

Phelps circled Damon slowly. "How long have you known Mr. Collins?"

"Over twenty years," Damon said. "We came up together. Hustling since we were teenagers."

"And when you were arrested with 15 kilos, how many were yours?"

"Seven," Damon answered. "Jason fronted the other eight."

"And that process went on for how long?"

"For years."

Gasps echoed in the courtroom. Jason's family looked at each other, whispering. Rosa looked frozen. Jason closed his eyes again.

Phelps smiled slightly. "And when you came home, what did Mr. Collins have waiting for you?"

"A brand-new SUV. Paid for. And a dump truck," Damon said.

"And why those gifts?"

"Because Jason thought I stayed solid. Thought I didn't snitch."

"But that wasn't true, was it?" Phelps pressed.

"No," Damon admitted. "I signed a proffer agreement. I testified in front of a grand jury."

Phelps sat down, smiling like the game was won.

Maxwell approached slowly. "Mr. Richards, how much time did you get knocked off your sentence?"

"Years," Damon admitted.

"How long have you been hustling?" Maxwell asked.

"Since I was eleven."

"Who introduced who to the game?"

"I did," Damon said. "Jason was heavy into sports. I brought him in."

Maxwell nodded. "The dump truck business you mentioned—how's it going?"

"Real good," Damon replied.

"And who helped you start that?"

"Jason. He didn't want me going back to the streets."

"In your own words—was Jason clean? Drug-free?"

"Yes, he was."

"Was he involved in the community?"

"Absolutely. He sponsored baseball, football, and basketball little leagues."

Maxwell paused, then rested his case.

Some jurors looked torn. Some leaned back in their chairs, conflicted. It was no longer a clear tale of crime—it was a story of betrayal, blurred loyalty, and friendships twisted into legal leverage.

The courtroom felt like a theater of ghosts. Jason Collins sat watching a man he once called family testify against him—not because he hated him, but because the system rewarded betrayal with freedom. The truth was no longer a question of right or wrong—it was a matter of who could live with what they'd done when the lights went off.

CHAPTER 42

Carlos sat quietly in the federal holding tank, his elbows resting on his knees, eyes fixed on the cold concrete floor. The buzz of fluorescent lights above mixed with the low hum of restless inmates nearby. His heart wasn't racing, but it was heavy. It's really heavy. He knew what was next—the stand.

As he waited, thoughts raced. His mind flipped through scenes like a dusty photo album. Flashback: he and Jason sitting in a dimly lit condo off Peachtree Street, stacks of cash surrounding them like walls. Jason sat cross-legged on the hardwood, a bill counter humming between them.

"You know Jorge approached me with better numbers," Jason had said, watching the machine spit neat bundles.

Carlos didn't even look up, just kept feeding hundreds into the counter. "I knew he wanted to cross me. You bringing in too much money. It takes five of his boys to move what you are doing."

Jason cracked a smile. "Me and you lock in, brother. Fuck the world. And Jorge backstabbing ass."

Carlos laughed. "You a real one. Not too many built like you."

They both laughed, throwing bills in the air like confetti. There had to be at least three million on the floor. Jason had eventually stood, stretched, and said, "I'm starving. We've been here for hours just counting."

Carlos tossed a bundle in the air and caught it. "That's a great thing."

Back in the tank, the door creaked open. His name was called. A guard stepped in and handed him a brown sack lunch before nodding to follow. Carlos didn't touch the food. His appetite was gone.

IN THE COURTROOM:

The air was thick with anticipation. Jason's mother Rosa sat stoically beside Princess's mom, Delores, who cradled baby Jamie. The rest of the family filled out the pews behind them, facing a mixture of concern, faith, and fatigue. Jason wasn't allowed to look back, but he could feel their eyes burning prayers into his back.

AUSA Phelps stood.

"The prosecution calls its next witness: Destiny Lovett."

She strutted in wearing heels too tall for court, but her presence was undeniable. The room shifted. Hair slicked back, tight black dress, the former dancer from Magic City took the stand.

"Miss Lovett," Phelps began, "Can you tell the court how you came to know the defendant, Mr. Collins?"

"They came every Monday night like clockwork," she said. "Him and his crew. Throwin' money like it grew on trees. Ten of thousands every time."

Phelps smiled. "Did you ever hear him speak about what he did for a living?"

"He said he owned trucking companies, real estate, but everybody knew the streets were his real job."

Maxwell stood for the cross.

"Miss Lovett, have you ever seen Mr. Collins with drugs?"

She blinked. "No."

"Have you ever received a wire transfer from him? A check? Anything outside tips?"

"No."

"So everything you're saying is based on assumptions?"

"No, it's based on lifestyle."

Maxwell leaned in. "So your professional opinion as an exotic dancer is what we're to rely on here today?"

The court chuckled lightly. The judge gave a stern look. Phelps frowned. Maxwell sat down.

Next, Phelps called Jason's jeweler to the stand. A well-dressed man in a tailored gray suit.

"Can you tell the court your professional relationship with Mr. Collins?"

"Jason's been my client for over a decade. He has spent over a million in cash."

"All cash?"

"All cash. Mostly watches. One of a kind. Chains."

Maxwell stood.

"Sir, are you aware that Mr. Collins and his wife have filed taxes for the past ten years, reporting over $700,000 annually?"

"I—I don't know his taxes. I know he paid me."

"In full? Ever bounce a payment?"

"Never."

"Thank you."

Phelps next called the owner of Capital City Motors.

"How did Mr. Collins pay for his vehicles?"

"Cash."

"What kind of vehicles?"

"Maybach. G-Wagon. Escalade. Off the lot, no lease."

"Suspicious to you?"

"Not when you make that kind of money."

Maxwell stood again.

"Did he ever tell you the money came from drugs?"

"No."

"Then why are you here?"

"Because I got subpoenaed."

Maxwell nodded. Then he returned to his table and clicked a remote.

A projection lit up on a screen: IRS tax records from the last decade. Filed jointly. Consistent income. $1.4 million reported in each of the last three years. Taxes paid. Paper trail airtight.

He stood before the jury.

"Ladies and gentlemen, there is a difference between assumption and evidence. There is a difference between lifestyle and legality. Do not be swayed by glitter and gossip. Jason Collins paid his dues, on time, in full, and legally."

Jason looked to his left where Carlos was now seated. Their eyes met for a brief moment. Carlos looked away.

The court was a stage. And like all great dramas, it demanded a villain. But when loyalty and betrayal stand shoulder to shoulder, it becomes harder to tell who is acting—and who is just surviving. Carlos wasn't ready to throw his life away, but the guilt draped over his shoulders like a lead vest. And as Jason stared forward, flanked by two federal marshals, the question lingered in the jury's mind:

Was he the kingpin they feared—or the scapegoat they needed?"
}

CHAPTER 43

The air in the hotel room was thick with smoke, bass-heavy music, and the kind of recklessness that made bad decisions seem like good ones. Rico sat in a high-backed leather chair, a thick blunt in one hand, a shot of tequila in the other. Two girls danced in front of him, topless, moving to the rhythm as if hypnotized. But Rico wasn't watching them. He was thinking.

The door swung open. Bud and Bay Bay walked in, both wearing dark hoodies and serious faces. Rico stood up and motioned for them to follow him to the backroom.

"Look," Rico said, closing the door behind them. "Y'all gotta make this go smooth as hell. Don't hurt anybody."

Bud smirked. "No problem. We just want the money. No blood."

Rico stepped in closer. "I'm dead serious. The boys over my house playin' with my son. Sierra there by herself. This can't get messy."

Bay Bay asked, "We kickin' the door in, or what?"

Rico shook his head. "Nah. Her car parked outside. The garage opens on sun vision. I peeped that the other day. Drake's car is still there too. Look, just get in, get the bag, and get out. Don't hurt her. She gon' give it up."

The three men shook hands.

Rico turned and stepped out of the room. He handed both dancers a few hundred dollars and told them to get dressed and leave. "Fun's over," he said. "Time for business."

Later that night, Bud and Bay Bay pulled up to Drake's house. They saw Drake's SUV parked in the driveway. The neighborhood was quiet. No kids playing. No dogs barking. Just silence.

Inside the house, Sierra was lying across the bed, music playing softly. She was relaxed, even smiling, until she heard the garage open. She sat up slowly. Something wasn't right. She reached into the nightstand and grabbed her Glock.

Drake always told her, "Keep all the lights on at night. That way, if somebody comes in, they won't know what room you are in."

She remembered.

Heavy footsteps moved up the stairs. Sierra took a deep breath and chambered a round. Her heart was steady. The first shadow came into view.

She didn't hesitate.

Three rapid shots rang out. The first one hit Bud in the chest, dropping him instantly. Bay Bay, halfway up the stairs, screamed and ducked. He fired blindly and ran back down as Sierra returned fire.

Then everything went silent.

Sierra moved slowly, stepping over Bud's body. Her hand was firm on the grip of the gun. She reached for her phone and called 911.

Then, she called the second number on the speed dial: Drake.

Inside federal prison, Drake was sitting in the TV room with Jason. They were talking about trial strategy when his phone buzzed. Drake stepped into the corner and answered.

"Hello?"

"Baby," Sierra whispered, "I'm lookin' at a dead body at the top of our stairs. Somebody broke in."

Drake clutched the phone. Panic took over his face.

Jason stood up. "Yo, what's wrong?"

Drake looked at him, face pale. "They tried to hit my crib. Sierra just killed somebody."

Jason clenched his fists. "Is she okay?"

"Yeah. She called the cops already. I told her to keep it tight, not say a word 'til her lawyer gets there."

Meanwhile, Bay Bay was in the back of a dark alley texting Rico.

Bay Bay: "Shit went wrong. Bud dead. Need a ride. Fast."

Rico stared at the message. Sweat ran down his neck. A million thoughts hit him at once.

He had set this up. Now one of his boys was dead, and Sierra had every right to talk. Everything just went from sweet to sour.

Some moments you can't walk back from. Rico thought this was a simple lick. But when blood hits the floor, the streets start talking. And when a woman protects her home like a soldier, even the darkest plans unravel. The fallout has begun the clock was ticking

Bay Bay leaned against the inside of a tinted sedan, his hands still shaking. Rico stood across from him in an empty lot behind an abandoned warehouse.

"Bay, what the fuck happened?" Rico snapped.

Bay Bay wiped sweat from his face, his eyes wide. "Man, we went in and all the lights was on. That threw us off. Didn't know where to start, so we headed upstairs. Shawty was waiting on us. Bud was first up—she dome him, man. Let off like a damn sharpshooter."

Rico blinked. "Drake used to take her to the gun range. Shoulda known."

"Who else knew about tonight?" Rico asked coldly.

"Nobody. To my knowledge," Bay Bay replied, voice low.

Rico nodded, lips pressed tight. Then, without a word, he turned and walked to a nearby dead-end street. He looked up and down, pulled out his Glock, and shot Bay Bay three times. The silence after was louder than the gunfire.

Back in his prison cell, Drake sat on the edge of the bunk, arms folded, deep in thought. His mind raced. Who would try to rob his family?

He picked up the phone and called Rico.

Rico answered quickly, his tone calm. "What's up, bro?"

At that same moment, he looked at Bud's lifeless body

Drake asked, "The boys having fun?"

"Yeah, man. We had pizza, wings, and video games. They tight tight."

Drake smiled. "Right. Let me speak to Lil Dee real quick. I need to ask him something."

Rico hesitated. "I just left. Just pulled off. I'll be pulling back up in five minutes."

Drake nodded slowly. "No worries. I'll just call his phone."

There was a pause.

"Yeah... yeah, do that," Rico muttered, knowing this was only going to spiral worse.

The tension was thick, and Drake felt it.

And somewhere deep in his gut, he knew: something was off.

The real storm hadn't even started yet.

CHAPTER 44

SMOKE AND SILENCE

Some wolves don't howl. They smile. But when the blood hits the floor, the silence in the aftermath screams louder than any gunshot.

Sierra sat frozen on the staircase, watching as officers moved around her home with cameras and evidence bags. Bud's body was still there, lifeless and facedown, a red pool surrounding him like a final goodbye. Everything had happened so fast. The door, the footsteps, the gunfire—and now the silence.

Tasha pulled up and jumped out the car, rushing to the front door.

"Sierra! What happened?!"

Sierra could barely speak. Her voice cracked. "I can't stay here anymore."

Tasha looked around, then asked, "Where are the boys?"

"Over at Rico's house."

Tasha's expression changed instantly. "Rico? Don't they all hang together? Have you told him?"

Sierra shook her head slowly. "No. Drake told me not to say anything."

Back inside the federal detention center, Drake and Jason sat in the corner of the dayroom.

"You think Rico sent them?" Jason asked.

Drake sighed. "Hard to tell. If anybody knew Sierra had the money, it was him. But he didn't need to take it. I would've given it to him."

202 | G H O S T D O P E

Jason leaned forward. "Man, I saw Dice on the stand yesterday. After that, I don't put anything past nobody. I told Princess to stay at her mama house 'til I get her a new crib. The bullshit hittin' the fan."

Drake nodded. "Glad I was taking Sierra to the gun range. She handled herself."

Jason said, "Only one way to play it. Get your brother. Get your boys. Sierra needs to leave Tampa ASAP."

"Got a little over half a mil in the house," Drake admitted. "Rest in safe deposit boxes and other spots."

Jason stared at him. "Don't trust nobody, not even your shadow."

Meanwhile, Rico sat on the couch at his townhouse. His head was spinning. The sound of NBA 2K came from the other room. The boys were playing, laughing.

Tanisha walked in, her phone still lit up in her hand. "Lou just called me. Said Bud's dead."

Rico turned slowly. "What?"

"She said her sister had to ID the body. Sounds like a robbery gone wrong."

Just then, the doorbell rang.

Rico opened the door. Hakeem stood there with a blank expression. "I'm here to get the boys."

"I thought they were spending the night," Rico said.

"Plans changed. Sis said she got something set up for them tomorrow. Sierra wants them home."

The boys came to the door, pleading.

"Uncle Rico, can we stay?" Lil Dee asked.

"Nah," Hakeem said. "Pack it up. Let's go."

Rico didn't say another word. He just watched.

His heart raced. Everything was falling apart.

He thought silence bought him time. But silence, in this world, only made the gun louder when it fired back. And now, Rico was hearing the click.

CHAPTER 45

LOYALTY ON TRIAL

Narration: Sometimes betrayal doesn't come from strangers. It comes from the ones who toasted with you, who smiled in your home, who knew your dreams—and watched them burn.

Rosa, Delores, and Princess sat in the cozy front room of Delores' home. The new baby slept peacefully in a bassinet beside them, wrapped in a pink blanket that read Jamie B.

A bottle of wine sat open on the table. Rosa poured another round as the conversation turned serious.

"You know Dice took the stand against Jay?" Princess said, her voice low, eyes fixed on the baby.

Delores shook her head slowly. "As much as Jay did for him and his family. All that loyalty... the whole time he was plotting."

Rosa clenched her wine glass. "That man ate at my table. I treated him like one of my own. Ain't no loyalty no more—just low down and dirty."

Delores nodded, sipping slowly. "I feel so bad for Jay. But I must admit—his lawyers are holding it down."

"They are," Rosa agreed. "And all these people who benefited when things were good? On the stand talkin' 'bout Jay always paid in cash. Like they didn't know. But guess what? They had receipts."

Delores raised her glass. "Hell yeah. Paid taxes on 1.4 million last three years. When they pulled those returns, the jury was shook. I believe Jay is gonna beat this."

Princess exhaled slowly. "The only one I'm nervous about is his Mexican friend. Carlos."

Meanwhile, Coach Teddy Love stood in the backyard, grilled off, beer half-empty in hand. Nikki, his wife, sat nearby on the deck, arms folded.

"What if you don't take the stand?" she asked.

Coach Love rubbed his head. "They said they'll hit me with money laundering and tax evasion."

Nikki looked at him hard. "Ain't this against the law? Teddy, they can't prove that money came from Jay's drug money. He got legit businesses. He wired it to you that money came from his bank account, right?"

"Right. But they said if they can show I knew where the money came from, I could still get charged."

Nikki took his hand. "I'm behind you. Whatever you decide. But what's your gut telling you?"

Coach Love stared off at the fading sun. "I hate to do it... but I might take the stand tomorrow.

At the Tampa police department, Sierra sat stiffly in a chair across from two detectives. Her lawyer, Ms. Monica Fields, sat beside her.

"Did you know the man you shot last night?" one detective asked, pushing a photo across the table.

Sierra glanced at it. "Yes. Bobby Jones."

"Was that the first time he'd been in your home?"

"No," Sierra answered plainly.

The detective leaned forward. "Did Drake Willis ever store drugs or cash at this residence?"

Monica raised a hand. "She's the victim here. Let's keep this clean and respectful."

The detective backed off slightly. "Just asking for context."

They asked a few more questions, then finally dismissed her. Sierra stood, nodded, and walked out, holding her composure until she reached the parking lot.

Rico sat in a dark room with Fat Clay, sipping from a Styrofoam cup. The weed smoke hung in the air.

"I told Bud to stay away from her," Rico said, shaking his head.

Fat Clay looked down. "Lil bro was hurting. Thought Drake left him for dead... but still, that move? On Sierra and Drake? Nah."

Rico shrugged. "I don't know who else was down."

Fat Clay looked over. "I just hope Drake doesn't come for revenge."

Rico let out a breath. "He has too much going on now. Bud dead. What revenge?"

Night had a way of peeling back the faces people wore in daylight. It was under moonlight truths got stripped down, loyalties tested, and betrayals echoed loudest. Inside a dim-lit cell, two men sat on hard benches—weathered but not broken. Jay and Drake, brothers by bond, not blood. Cuffed by the feds but not by fear.

Drake rubbed the bridge of his nose, tension pulsing behind his eyes.

"Man," he muttered, "I had plans for Rico and Bud to run my business. Keep the wheels turning. Thought we were solid."

Jay leaned forward, his voice low but heavy. "Rico might've been cool at one point... but Bud wouldn't have made no move like that without clearing it. Ain't no way. You know what that means."

Drake nodded, jaw tight. "Only three people knew where Sierra was... me, Bud, and Rico. Now Bud is dead, Sierra almost got smoked, and Rico is too quiet."

Jay's eyes locked with his. "That silence says everything. Ain't no loyalty in long money if trust gets broken. You feel it in your gut for a reason. Don't ignore that."

Drake sat back, exhaling. "I gotta protect Sierra and the kids. Movers coming tomorrow. I'm packing them up outta Tampa. Fast. Quiet."

Jay looked down, rubbed his wrists, then backed up. "Good. Move them like your freedom depends on it—'cause it does."

A beat passed.

"Tomorrow I face Carlos in court. Crazy, ain't it?" Jay continued, tone darker now. "Same dude we used to call brother. Broke bread with. Built empires with. Now he's up next pointing fingers, just like Dice."

Drake shook his head. "What do you think he's getting for it? A shorter bid? A cell with a window?"

Jay laughed, dry. "Maybe. But he gon' carry that in his soul forever. I can sit in this box knowing I held it down. I ain't fold. I ain't snake nobody."

Drake's voice dropped. "That's why I say, even if we lose time... we can't lose honor."

Jay nodded slowly. "Real ones know—the code ain't written on paper. It's etched in who you are."

And so in the quiet shadows of a prison cell, two men did what most forget—held to the code. Even as the world around them cracked, even as brothers betrayed and blood boiled, they chose the hardest thing: to stay solid. Tomorrow brought new battles. But tonight, they spoke like terminology, and enriched for storytelling.

CHAPTER 46

The stakes had never been higher. Inside the packed courtroom, time itself seemed to hold its breath. Friends, family, even former foes filled the benches—everyone chasing answers, closure, or chaos. Some came to support. Others came to see blood.

The moment the prosecution called their next witness, a slow ripple moved across the room.

"All rise," the clerk called as Judge Michael returned. The chatter stilled, and the real war began.

AUSA Phelps rose from her table like a predator ready to finish her prey.

"Your Honor, the government calls Theodore Love to the stand."

Gasps echoed softly as Coach Teddy Love entered the courtroom, his face tight with regret. His once-proud gait was dimmed by shame. From the benches, a few old coaching colleagues muttered under their breath, "This some bullshit..."

Jason squinted in confusion. He leaned toward his attorney, Maxwell, whispering low.

"How the hell did we miss Teddy's name? Man ain't been in the game in over seven years."

Maxwell flipped through his file, already shaking his head.

"They added him this morning, Jason. Slide it in under a sealed amendment. No time to counter."

Jason's expression darkened. Around them, even the jury looked stunned.

The murmuring grew louder. Judge Michael struck the gavel. "Quiet in the courtroom. Now."

Coach Love sat stiffly, clearly torn. Phelps approached slowly, her tone clinical, calculated.

"Mr. Love, you and the defendant… you go back some years, correct?"

Teddy nodded, "Yes, ma'am. A little over twenty. We coached together, ran camps, youth sports—"

"And a box truck company," Phelps added, cutting in smoothly. "Four vehicles, correct?"

"Yes."

She turned toward the projector, clicked a remote. A large statement filled the screen—Teddy's signed confession from eight years ago. Gasps fluttered again.

"Do you recognize this document, Mr. Love?"

Teddy hesitated. "Yes."

"Would you mind reading the first two lines aloud?"

Teddy's voice cracked slightly as he read: "The drugs found at my residence belonged to Jason Collins. I was holding them for him."

The room exhaled like a punch had just landed.

Maxwell stood immediately. "Objection, Your Honor. This statement is dated over five years ago. The statute of limitations on this isolated offense should apply. It's stale."

Judge Michael looked toward Phelps.

She didn't flinch. "Your Honor, under Federal Rule 404(b) and Rule 801(d)(2), the government may present prior bad acts and out-of-court statements as part of a broader criminal enterprise. This falls under relevant conduct in furtherance of a continuing conspiracy—U.S. v. Beechum supports this."

Judge Michael leaned back. "Objection overruled. Proceed."

Phelps turned back toward the jury. "Mr. Love, to be clear, you're telling this court that not only did you store narcotics for Mr. Collins... you also handled and hid money on his behalf?"

"Yes," Teddy admitted, not making eye contact with Jason.

"Over what period?"

"Several years. Not continuously—but yes, there were times."

Jason's mother Rosa turned her head in disbelief. Delores gripped Princess's hand tightly. Whispers rose across the courtroom.

Jason sat still. Calm on the outside. Erupting on the inside.

Phelps paced slowly, letting it all marinate.

"No further questions, Your Honor," she said before sitting down.

Maxwell rose and approached the stand, measured, controlled.

"Coach Love," he said with a faint scoff, "how long ago was this alleged drug-holding incident?"

"Eight years."

"Eight years," Maxwell repeated, "and you never spoke about it—not once—until now, when you were threatened with money laundering and tax evasion, correct?"

Teddy looked down. "Yes."

"You were granted limited immunity for your testimony?"

"Yes."

"Isn't it true, sir, that the money Mr. Collins gave you came from a legitimate business? A youth sports program, two nightclubs, and three licensed barbershops?"

"I... I can't speak to all that."

"But you accepted the money," Maxwell said sharply. "Even deposited it, filed it as investment income?"

Teddy nodded slowly.

Maxwell turned to the jury.

"Ladies and gentlemen, the government wants you to believe that Jason Collins is some shadow kingpin. Yet their star witnesses are people who benefitted from his success. Who partied with him, coached with him, broke bread at his table. And when pressed— when they got caught—they folded to save their own necks."

He turned back to Teddy.

"Did Jason Collins ever ask you to sell drugs?"

"No."

"Did he ever threaten you?"

"No."

"Did he ever once fail to show up for the kids you coached together?"

"No."

"No further questions."

Judge Michael gave a nod.

Phelps stood slowly, glanced at her notes, and said coldly, "The government calls Carlos Ramirez."

The courtroom stiffened.

Jason's head turned. Carlos entered in khakis and a button-up shirt, trying to look like a civilian. For a moment, their eyes met. Jason's stare was steel. Carlos looked away.

No words were spoken. But the betrayal screamed loud.

In the end, the courtroom was more than wood and walls—it was a battleground where loyalty died and silence had a price. As Jason braced for Carlos to speak, the weight of the past two decades pressed on him like a freight train. What once felt like brotherhood now smelled like war. Every man on the stand wasn't just testifying—they were burying memories for immunity. And Jason knew, the worst part wasn't the time they'd try to give him. It was the ones who helped them do it.

The courtroom was still. You could hear the shifting of a suit jacket, the scribble of a pen. Eyes locked in as the next witness took the stand—Carlos Ramirez. The man who once toasted to brotherhood on foreign sands was now sworn in under oath, eyes heavy, heart unreadable.

PHELPS approached slowly, building anticipation with every step.

AUSA PHELPS (calm, deliberate):

"Mr. Ramirez… Can you tell the court how you first met Jason Collins?"

CARLOS (voice steady):

"I met Jason at a luxury car dealership. He was buying a brand-new, his-and-hers Range Rover. Custom. All cash."

The courtroom stirred.

PHELPS:
"And what happened during that encounter?"

CARLOS (nodding slowly):

"I told him I had thirty kilos in a secret compartment… $16,000 per key. Show him a sample."

PHELPS:
"And Mr. Collins' reaction?"

CARLOS:
"He made a call right there. Within the hour, someone pulled up with half a million dollars cash. No hesitation."

Narration:

You could feel the oxygen leave the room. The jury, spectators—even the stenographer paused for a beat. It wasn't testimony. It was cinema. Like watching a godfather movie unfold live. Raw, unapologetic.

PHELPS (leaning in):

"What happened after that?"

CARLOS:

"For the next eight years, we made millions together. We bought a trucking company—used it to move dope and wash money. Jason was the brain. I had Mexico. He had Atlanta and the routes."

PHELPS:

"And the semi-truck pulled over in Augusta, Georgia—what was its destination?"

CARLOS (matter-of-fact):

"My warehouse."

Narration:

Eyes turned to Jason. His jaw was tight, expression unreadable. But his hand twitched—once—on the table.

Suddenly, pictures flickered across the courtroom projector. Bright beach sun. Smiling faces. Frozen memories that now burned with betrayal

PRINCESS'S FLASHBACK

Princess sat frozen as the pictures scrolled—Jason, their two boys, Carlos and Leticia with their daughter and son, Drake, his wife and boys. They were all there—poolside at a beachfront resort, music in the background, laughter in the air, drinks flowing, a chef grilling fresh food, the smell of joy and loyalty thick in the air.

Princess remembered the moment—Carlos with his arm around both Jason and Jay, raising his glass.

CARLOS (in flashback, laughing):

"These two right here? The best thing ever happened to me. I'll kill or be killed for 'em. My brothers for life!"

Leticia, beaming, leaned over to Princess, wine glass in hand.

LETICIA:

"He hasn't smiled like this in years. We're family, Princess. Nothing will ever come between us."

Narration:

But now... something had. That "nothing" had become everything.

Back to the courtroom—the projector now frozen on a photo of Jason, Carlos, and Jay in suits, grinning, a snapshot of loyalty that had already been buried.

MAXWELL stepped forward for cross-examination.

MAXWELL (firm, methodical):

"Mr. Ramirez, are you legally in the United States?"

CARLOS (quietly):

"No."

MAXWELL:

"Who had the connection to Mexico?"

CARLOS:

"Me."

MAXWELL:

"And yet, despite all that power, all that connection… you're here today as a cooperating government witness. Tell this court—how did that happen?"

CARLOS (pausing):

"Jorge set me up."

MAXWELL (pacing):

"Set you up how?"

CARLOS:
"He flipped. Fed me to the DEA. They raided a warehouse. I was looking at over 30 years."

MAXWELL (leaning on the jury box):

"Thirty years... but you're not serving thirty years, are you, Mr. Ramirez?"

CARLOS:
"No."

MAXWELL:
"In fact, instead of wearing a jumpsuit for the rest of your life, you worked out a deal, correct?"

CARLOS:
"Yes."

MAXWELL (to jury):

"So here we have Carlos Ramirez. An undocumented trafficker. A man who smuggled poison into this country. A man who built a criminal empire from Mexican soil to American streets—and now… now, he points fingers to save himself."

The courtroom hung in that truth. Carlos, once the life of the party, the architect of celebration, was now the mouthpiece of federal salvation. Some jurors shifted. Others stared at Jason with a mixture of curiosity and doubt.

Maxwell didn't need to scream. His words—clean, sharp—cut through the illusion. This wasn't loyalty. It was leverage.

The judge called for recess.

Chapter 47

THE SUMMATION

The courtroom was heavy. Still. No more witnesses. No more evidence. Just eyes on two people now—Maxwell, and AUSA Phelps.

Jason Collins sat motionless. His suit looked tailored, but his eyes looked worn. Behind him, family. Beside him, silence. Ahead of him… fate.

The judge looked over his glasses.

"Counselors, we'll hear closing arguments. The government may proceed."

AUSA PHELPS stood. Adjusted her jacket. Took a slow breath. Then approached the jury.

AUSA PHELPS (Prosecution) Closing Argument:

"Ladies and gentlemen of the jury…

You've heard the names. You've seen the faces. You've followed the money.

And now you've heard the truth.

This case isn't about hearsay or hustlers spinning stories in alleyways. This case is about structure. About power. About organization. Jason Collins didn't just participate in a conspiracy—he built it. He ran it. He profited from it."

She pointed to the projection still frozen behind her—Jason, Jay, and Carlos at the beach.

"Do not be fooled by the smiles in these photos. They were not just friends on vacation. They were partners in a multi-million-dollar criminal enterprise that spanned states and nations.

Carlos Ramirez didn't just testify because he wanted to hurt anyone—he testified because the truth finally caught up with him. Jason Collins made the calls. He coordinated the shipments. He laundered the money. He fronted the dope. He built a public image of a businessman while burying kilos behind semi-truck walls.

And when witnesses took the stand and said Jason gifted them dump trucks, SUVs, homes, and paid their debts—you know why?

Because that's how you buy silence.

This isn't a case about loyalty. This is a case about accountability. And today, the law must hold Jason Collins accountable.

You don't get to sponsor little league games by day and ship cocaine by night and call it community service.

You don't get to flash a smile and erase a ledger.

And you don't get to hide behind family photos while destroying other families for profit.

We ask you—on behalf of the United States of America—to return the only just verdict: Guilty. Thank you."

Jason's mother lowered her head. Princess gripped her hands so tight her knuckles turned pale. Maxwell stood, slow and focused, and walked to the front like a soldier facing a firing squad—knowing his armor was words, and only words.

MAXWELL (Defense) Closing Argument:

"Ladies and gentlemen…

You just heard a hell of a story. Dramatic. Clean. Tied up with a bow.

But here's the problem: the government is selling you a movie—when they were supposed to prove a case.

Let's step back.

How many witnesses did they parade up here? Seven? Eight? All of them with one thing in common—they were getting something in return. A sentence reduction. A plea deal. Protection. Green cards. All bought with the same currency: testimony.

The prosecution says Jason Collins is a criminal mastermind. But where's the hard proof? No wiretap. No recorded drug deal. No fingerprints on kilos. No video of cash hand-offs.

You heard from a jeweler, a stripper, a car salesman. Since when did buying luxury items with your own money become a crime?

The IRS confirmed Jason and his wife paid over $1.4 million in taxes in just the last three years. That's not drug dealer behavior—that's transparency.

And let's talk about Carlos Ramirez—their star witness. A man who smuggled drugs across borders, broke federal laws for nearly a decade, and is not even a legal citizen of the country he's testifying in. And he's the man they want you to trust?

What's his reward? A sentence cut from 30 years to possibly five.

He's not telling the truth—he's telling a transaction.

Jason Collins is not perfect. He's made choices. But none of them prove what the government wants you to believe.

He didn't choose the streets over his family—he chose to provide for them. He didn't fund violence—he funded youth sports, Black businesses, construction companies.

You want to say he was around people who did dirt? Fine. But being in the kitchen doesn't make you the cook.

I ask you today—not just to follow the law, but to follow your instinct. Your wisdom. Your discernment.

Because once you give a man's life away to the system—you don't get to take it back.

Don't convict him of guilt by association. Convict only if they've proven their case beyond a reasonable doubt. And I submit to you: they have not.

Jason Collins deserves justice too. And that justice is a Not Guilty verdict.

Thank you."

The courtroom was still again.

Not a phone buzzed. Not a pen scratched. Not a whisper was heard.

The judge called for a break. Jury to deliberate. And outside, beyond the windows, the sun began to fall.

Inside, a man's entire world now balanced on twelve minds behind a wooden door.

This wasn't about who smiled in photos. This was about who would survive the truth—and what price betrayal truly cost.

CHAPTER 48

THE WEIGHT OF TWELVE

Narration: The door to the jury room shut with a solid click, and the outside world disappeared. Twelve people, handpicked from different walks of life, now held Jason Collins' fate in their hands. They didn't know him. Not really. But for the next however-many-hours, they'd know every word ever spoken about him.

Inside, the air was heavy. Not from heat, but from the sheer weight of it all.

Jury Foreman (Mrs. Evelyn Trask, age 61) cleared her throat and opened the discussion.

"Let's begin. We've all heard the testimony, seen the evidence. It's time to talk. Where does everyone stand?"

A middle-aged Black man named George Winters, a retired corrections officer, raised his hand first. "I'm leaning toward guilt. Too many people said the same thing about Jason. The dump trucks, the cars, the way he took care of folks who went to prison—"

"But that doesn't make him a criminal," interrupted Samantha Lee, a soft-spoken woman in her 30s, a single mother and retail manager. "Paying people's rent and sponsoring sports teams? That ain't proof. That's love. That's community."

A younger white man, Travis Green, tattoos peeking from under his dress shirt sleeves, leaned back in his chair. "Carlos Ramirez lost me. How are you gonna be a career smuggler, not even legal in the U.S., and now you up here playing federal witness? He told a good story, but he told it to save his own ass."

Mrs. Trask nodded slowly. "I agree. Carlos had every reason to lie. But what about Coach Love? He said Jason gave him large transfers and didn't explain where the money came from."

"Coach Love was scared," countered Linda Cruz, a school counselor. "They threatened him with time. He didn't want to take the stand, remember? His body language said it all. He was trying to protect himself."

Narration: Back and forth they went. Over Jason's wife. Over the taxes. Over the box trucks. Over the damn SUV.

One woman began to cry quietly. A young Asian juror, Mei Lin, wiped her eyes and whispered, "What if we get this wrong? What if he really didn't do it, and we ruined his life?"

The foreman looked around. "We need clarity. Let's go witness by witness."

They dissected Damon Richards' testimony next.

"He said Jason gave him a dump truck and a new SUV. Because he didn't snitch," said George. "But he was snitching all along. Said Jason fronted him eight keys. That part stuck with me."

"It stuck with me too," said Samantha. "But did anyone ever confirm that with actual proof? Damon got a deal too, remember."

"He had to, or face a long sentence," Mei Lin said softly.

Then came the stripper. The jeweler. The car dealer. Names blurred. Faces replayed.

Travis: "Everybody who testified was paid or promised something. Every single one."

George: "But the money? The lifestyle? That doesn't come from selling cookies."

Linda: "He had a tax record. Over a million a year, documented. We can't convict off vibes."

Narration: Time passed. Hours blurred. Sandwiches and coffee were delivered, untouched.

Then the bailiff knocked and passed them a message.

Judge Michael's Note: The court expects a verdict today. You may deliberate further, but I remind you this trial has consumed weeks of resources. The public and this court need resolution.

The weight doubled.

Narration (cut to hallway outside

CHAPTER 49

THE WEIGHT OF WAITING

Outside the courtroom doors, the lobby of the federal courthouse in downtown Atlanta felt more like a chapel than a hallway. The sterile white floors echoed with the creak of shoes, the murmur of prayers, and the faint hum of fluorescent lights that had watched too many families crumble under the weight of federal justice.

A cluster of family members stood against the wall beneath a mounted television that played the news on mute. The screen showed unrelated headlines—gas prices rising, a local school shooting vigil, a stock market crash—but no one was watching. Their eyes were on each other, or closed in silent pleading.

Princess stood near a column, wearing all black—a tailored blazer, slacks, and low heels. Oversized sunglasses covered her eyes, but her posture was statuesque. Her lips didn't tremble. Her knees didn't buckle. She held her baby girl in one arm, swaying her gently, whispering a lullaby while texting a babysitter on her phone. On her other wrist, she still wore the bracelet Jason gave her when their first child was born. She hadn't taken it off since.

Beside her sat Rosa, Jason's mother, in a burgundy shawl and cream dress. Her Bible was open in her lap, lips moving in silent prayer. Her fingers trembled every time someone walked by in a suit, fearing it might be the clerk with the verdict. She looked up, finally whispering to Princess, "They think just 'cause we are from the Southside, we don't know how to stand with grace. But baby… this ain't our first storm. And it won't be our last."

Princess nodded, emotion catching in her throat. "I just want him home, Ma," she said softly. "I just want our family back."

Across the lobby, Jason's younger cousin Ant was pacing, AirPods in, whispering to a friend about what was happening. "They are trying to railroad my cousin, bro. Real talk. Had folks up there testifying just to save their own skin. That ain't justice. That's chess with people's lives."

Two of Jason's childhood friends sat on a bench near the elevators. One of them, Raheem, was crying silently into his hoodie. The other, Darius, stared at his hands. "We used to hoop every Sunday," Darius mumbled. "Now we are lucky if we get to see each other through glass."

Down the hall, Delores had gathered four women into a prayer circle. She held Rosa's hand, her own voice steady and forceful. "Father God, we don't pray for miracles. We pray for truth. For protection over Jason. For protection over Princess and their babies. For Your justice—not theirs."

A few paces away, Jay's brother Marcus was on the phone with their attorney's paralegal. "No updates?" he asked, frustration leaking into his voice. "We've been waiting six hours. What are they doing, flipping a coin?"

Just then, one of the guards came through the hallway doors. Everyone paused. Silence struck the room like a sudden cold front. But the guard only nodded at a colleague and walked past.

The tension returned like a noose slowly tightening.

Princess walked toward Rosa and bent slightly to hand the baby over to her grandmother. "You okay?" Rosa asked, taking the infant gently, rocking her.

"I think I'm too numb to cry now," Princess replied. "I didn't sleep. Been staring at the ceiling wondering how a man can build a life, give back, pay taxes, invest in the community... and still end up here. Like none of it matters."

Rosa looked her dead in the eye. "It does matter. You hear me? They can lie on paper. They can twist stories in court. But the truth is don't go to sleep just 'cause a jury is confused. God sees all this. God don't miss."

A cousin walked over with her phone in her hand. "They just posted about Carlos on Facebook. People dragging him. Said he was calling Jason his 'brother' in Cancun but now he is the reason this man might not see the outside for twenty years."

Princess shook her head slowly. "That trip was sacred. Our kids played together. His wife told me we were 'family.' And he turned around and gave them a movie script. Made Jason look like El Chapo."

Rosa's voice dropped low but stayed firm. "The devil always wears familiar faces."

Another hour passed.

A marshal opened the courtroom doors, stepping halfway out. Everyone flinched. "Still deliberating," he said. "The judge said he'll check in again at six."

The clock on the wall read 5:12 PM.

One by one, people began to sit, fold hands, or take walks just to breathe. The elevator dinged softly as others came and went. A cousin returned with two vending machine sodas and passed one to Rosa. She took it with a smile, her first in hours.

Princess stood at the far end of the lobby, looking out the wide courthouse window. The skyline of Atlanta stretched before her—drenched in summer haze, glass buildings glowing in gold hour light. Somewhere out there, her house still stood. Her children's rooms still had toys scattered across the floors. And her husband's cologne still lingered on the pillow.

She wiped her face and whispered, "If you coming home, God... I need to know."

And then, from the back of the lobby, came a low rumble—an energy, a shift. The double doors opened again.

This time, it was the bailiff.

"Ladies and gentlemen... we have a verdict."

The breath left the lobby. Hearts jumped into throats. Mothers squeezed hands tighter. Friends who hadn't spoken in years stood shoulder to shoulder, bound by fate. In one collective motion, the group stood.

Outside the courtroom was a symphony of prayer and pulse. And inside, a man's future balanced on the edge of a single word: Guilty... or Not.

The hallway went still. But the storm was just beginning.

CHAPTER 50

OPERATION THREE KINGS

Opening

Three kings, three stories, three heavy crowns—Drake, Carlos, and Jason. Each in a different cell. Each with the same silence smothering them. The courtroom might have gone still, but their minds refused.

DRAKE – HOLDING CELL B3

Drake sat on the edge of the metal bunk, elbows on his knees, eyes staring at the concrete floor like it owed him answers.

DRAKE (thinking aloud): "All the bricks I moved, all the deals I made, I told myself it was for them boys. That I was building an empire. But I built a trap... and put myself in it. I thought I was smart. That I knew the codes. Loyalty. Respect. No snitching. No folding. But look where those codes landed us. Bud dead. Rico is quiet. Sierra almost got killed. I used to think we were kings. Now I'm wondering if we were just pawns the whole time."

He stood up, pacing slowly, pulling out a wrinkled photo of his sons.

"And my boys... they don't need no street legend. They need a damn father. The world taught me how to be a hustler, not a man. But if I get one more shot... one more breath of real air... I'm changing that. Even if I have to crawl back into their lives piece by piece."

CARLOS – FEDERAL TRANSFER CELL A1

Carlos sat on the bench, chains still around his ankles, hands folded like prayer. But there was no religion in his silence.

CARLOS (thinking aloud): "I was the plug. The pipeline. I moved more keys than a piano store. And for what? For pesos that turned to prison. For love that turned to betrayal. Jorge set me up. Feds promised thirty years and smiled like they were offering salvation. So I talked. Told them everything. Painted the picture. Yeah, I lied in color. But what choice did I have?"

He leaned back, eyes flickering toward the door.

"Jason looked me in the eyes and called me family. I stood next to him on the beach, toasted to forever with our kids playing in the sand. But forever doesn't mean shit in this life. Not when you're caught. Not when you got chains around your soul."

His voice cracked now.

"I ain't just betrayed him. I betrayed

THE VERDICT APPROACHES

Jason sat alone in the cold metal holding cell beneath the courthouse, elbows resting on his knees, chained hands clasped together like he was still praying. His mind wasn't pacing—his heart was. The echoes of everything he had built, lost, protected, and destroyed swirled around him like ghosts whispering in the silence.

Jason (inner monologue):

Eight years ago, I was on the beach with my sons and my brothers. My girl smiled like she didn't have a care in the world. Drake's boys were playing with mine, Carlos had his daughter in his lap, and we were kings. We laughed like nothing could touch us...

He blinked slowly, forcing back the sting behind his eyes. The hum of the fluorescent light above him felt like a countdown clock. A marshal walked past the bars without saying a word.

Jason (inner monologue):

I didn't ask for this war. But I damn sure didn't run from it. I took care of people. Fed families. Put kids through college. But now? Now I'm just a name on a docket—Jason Lee Collins vs. The United States of America.

He chuckled to himself. A bitter, quiet laugh. He'd been a businessman, a father, a silent investor, a protector, a ghost in the system. But here—today—he was just a number in chains.

He thought about Dice, about Carlos, about Coach Love, all the ones who flipped. And then he thought about Sierra, about his sons, about Princess standing tall in court with sunglasses covering her pain but not her power. About Rosa, praying louder than the choir back home in Oakland.

Jason (inner monologue):

I didn't fold. I didn't point. Even when they brought out photos, wire taps, stacks of discovery… I kept it solid. So whatever comes through that door next, I'mma wear it. Like a man. Like a king. Like a father who still got people counting on him.

The clink of keys at the door snapped him out of his thoughts.

A deep voice followed: "Let's go. The jury's ready."

Jason stood slowly. Adjusted his suit jacket. Closed his eyes for one second—just one—and then stepped forward.

COURTROOM – TENSE SILENCE

The room was packed. Princess sat next to Rosa, both holding onto one another's hands like they were holding up the world.

Family members sat scattered—some crying, some stoic, others staring at the jury like they could read their souls.

Maxwell stood as the judge walked in. Jason entered behind him, led by two marshals who unshackled his wrists as he sat beside his attorney.

Judge Michael leaned forward.

"Mr. Foreman, has the jury reached a verdict?"

The foreman, a bald middle-aged Black man in a navy suit, stood.

"We have, Your Honor."

"Please pass it to the clerk."

A hush swept through the courtroom like a sudden change in wind. You could hear Princess exhale. Rosa bowed her head. Jason sat upright, jaw locked.

The clerk stood. Unfolded the paper slowly.

"In the case of the United States vs. Jason Lee Collins…"

One beat. Two.

CHAPTER 51

HUNG BUT NOT FREE

There are verdicts that shake a courtroom. And then there are verdicts that silence one. This was the latter.

Jason stood still, heart pounding like a war drum. The jury had just handed over their decision. Eyes darted across the room. The family held hands. Rosa was clutching her necklace. Princess sat frozen, her sunglasses unable to hide the tear gliding down her cheek.

The judge looked toward the foreman.

"Mr. Foreman, have you reached a unanimous verdict on all counts?"

The man cleared his throat. "Your Honor, we have a verdict on some counts... but we are hung on Count One: Conspiracy to distribute."

A pause. A shift in the room. Heads turned. People whispered. Maxwell turned slowly to Jason, eyes steady.

Judge Michael leaned forward. "On Count One, to be clear, this is a hung jury?"

"Yes, Your Honor. We could not reach a unanimous decision."

The judge sighed, pinched his eyes shut for a moment, and then nodded.

"Very well. The court acknowledges a partial verdict. On the remaining counts..."

He read down the line: Not guilty. Not guilty. Not guilty.

The room erupted.

Princess gasped and clutched Rosa. A shout came from the back. Maxwell closed his eyes with the quiet relief of a man who'd been on the brink. Jason's knees nearly buckled.

Judge Michael slammed his gavel. "Order in the court!"

The gavel struck again. "Mr. Collins, due to the hung count, you will remain in custody pending retrial on Count One."

Jason's smile faltered. His chest stopped rising. He looked at Maxwell.

"What does that mean? I thought I won."

Maxwell turned, voice calm but firm. "You won... but not the war. That one count—the conspiracy—that's what Phelps was banking on. Since the jury couldn't agree, the government gets to retry you on that charge."

Jason's face hardened. "So what now? I stay locked up?"

Maxwell nodded. "For now, yes. But listen to me—this is a win. It means at least some of those jurors didn't buy what Carlos and the rest were selling. You get one more hung jury on this and they may dismiss. Or we go for a not guilty. Either way, the pressure is on them now."

Behind them, Phelps stood stiffly, face like stone. She gathered her files, lips pressed thin. She turned to her second chair and whispered, "We're retrying him. And next time, I want Carlos to be tighter. No loopholes. No emotions. We bury him."

Maxwell glanced back at her and smirked. "She's pissed. That's good. Means she felt it."

Jason nodded slowly, looking over at his family. Princess gave him a hopeful smile. Rosa held her hands high in prayer. The rest of the supporters were hugging and wiping away tears.

Jason closed his eyes.

Jason (inner monologue): I didn't walk out those doors... not yet. But I walked out of hell with my head high. They didn't break me. And now I know something I didn't before—they can't all see me as guilty. Somebody in that jury room saw a man... not just a case file.

Narration: Hope doesn't come easy in a federal courtroom. But when it does—it lights a fire in every chained soul. Jason wasn't free. But he wasn't buried either. And that made all the difference.

The battle would continue. But now... Jason had seen the cracks.

And Phelps had seen the resistance.

Game on.

OTHER BOOKS BY TIERRE FORD